Lavender Lane

Christina Jones

Chapter One
The Family

'When's this darned thing going to start?' Bob Phillips blew on his hands and stamped his feet. 'Is there any chance of me sloping off for a cuppa before they get going?'

'No!' chorused the women on either side of him.

As they looked at each other and laughed. Bob glared at his wife and his mother and then grinned ruefully.

'OK. You're the experts, but I'm freezing to death here. I don't know how you stand it week after week.'

'Thermal underwear.' Cicely Phillips was seventy-five but admitted to sixty. 'And good fur-lined boots. And maybe a tot of rum before setting out!' she finished, laughing at her son.

'Anyway, once the race starts, it gets so exciting you don't have time to think about the cold!' his wife put in. 'Oh, what's happening now?'

'The front car's stalled,' Cicely said knowledgeably. 'They'll probably all get out and stretch their legs until it's started again ...'

Bob groaned. He'd gone along to the stock car racing under protest. His wife and his mother had both become keen fans since Mitchell had become involved – even though Bob kept telling them it was no sport for a lady. In return they had informed him icily that it was exciting, and that he didn't know what he was missing.

Bob sighed. He knew that only too well – he was missing a rare Saturday afternoon off.

As the wind howled across the track, small groups of

stalwarts snuggled further into their coats and shoved their hands deep into their pockets. The corrugated tin roof of the so-called stadium rattled dolefully under the onslaught.

Cicely and Amy didn't seem to notice the cold. Their eyes were glowing with pride as Mitch uncurled himself from his car and leaned against it, talking to one of the other drivers.

'He reminds me of your father.' Cicely nudged Bob. 'He was tall and broad-shouldered like Mitchell. And a bit of a daredevil, too.'

'Mother!' Bob shook his head. 'Dad was a vicar! I hardly think that's an apt description.'

'Ah, but he had a pilot's licence!' Cicely's eyes grew misty at the memory. 'That's where I fell in love with him, you know, up in the clouds. He literally swept me off my feet. It was so romantic! He was dreamy and gentle but in that plane he was daring and dashing … And what girl could resist an invitation for a jaunt in a plane?'

'I could.' Amy pulled a face at her mother-in-law. 'I don't like flying now, let alone in the days when they were held together with string!'

'You always were a bit of a rebel.' Bob smiled fondly at his mother. 'After all, how many vicars' wives rode motorbikes and took a job in a shop? You must have been the bane of the bishop's life. I reckon that's where Mitchell gets it from.'

'I do hope so.' Cicely beamed. 'After all, your other two are very straitlaced in comparison, aren't they?'

'Different,' Amy said gently, thinking of Matt and Megan. 'I think they're both more dedicated to the business than Mitchell is, but they've had their moments.'

She looked across at the drivers again and saw that Mitchell had removed his helmet. He certainly was something of a heartbreaker.

Matt, at twenty-eight their older son, was solid and reliable, with a friendly face and easy-going personality. Megan, twenty-five this year, showed characteristics of both her brothers, and was probably more sensible than either of them.

'Is that one of his mates he's talking to?' Bob squinted. 'Young Luke, is it? I can't tell. They all look the same in those overalls and helmets. They seem to be getting on very well.'

They certainly did, Amy thought, but the driver laughing at some joke Mitchell had made wasn't tall enough to be Luke. She felt a vague sense of foreboding.

'I don't think it's Luke, Bob. He doesn't drive in the races, does he? He just comes along and helps out with the mechanical bits.'

'Is anybody working for me this afternoon?' Bob grinned at his wife. 'We're all here. Luke and Mitchell are on the track. Matt is at home with Sally – and goodness knows what Megan's doing. Is anyone driving a Lavender cab?'

'Plenty.' Amy reassured him. 'The business won't go bust just because the Phillips family has taken a day off!'

Lavender Cabs was Bob and Amy's livelihood. It had grown, through three generations, into a thriving taxi and garage business. The small market town of Appleford was close enough to Oxford to attract tourists, and the taxis made a good living.

The garage which adjoined the Phillipses' sprawling bungalow in Lavender Lane was also a money-spinner, still offering the friendly family service it had when Amy's grandparents had set it up in the thirties.

'Oh, good! I think the race is going to start,' Cicely pointed out.

'Thank goodness for that.' Bob's feet had gone numb. 'Let's just see him write off yet another car and then we can go home and have a cuppa.'

Cicely glared at him. 'Philistine!'

Amy just gave him a reproachful look. She knew full well that Mitch had caused Bob more headaches than Matt and Megan put together, but she couldn't help loving this

3

wayward youngest son.

Mitch had thrown in college two years ago, when he was nineteen, to embark on a round-Europe backpacking trip. Amy had had grave doubts, and Bob had been furious, but aided and abetted by Cicely, Mitch had gone.

He'd returned, broke and suntanned, six months ago, full of hair-raising tales, and with an assumption that he'd just slot into the family business somewhere.

He helped out in the garage, and had soon become friends with Luke, Lavender Cabs' mechanic. It was Luke who had introduced Mitchell to stock cars.

'Just who is he talking to?' Bob tapped Amy's arm. 'They're – um – very close together, aren't they?'

Amy nodded, fearing the worst.

'They probably have to get close to hear what the other's talking about,' she said lamely. 'With the helmets and the noise and everything …'

'They seem to have realised that,' Cicely pointed out. 'Mitchell's friend is removing his helmet – oh, my goodness!'

Amy's heart sank. The long blonde hair cascading down from the helmet didn't belong to any man.

Jacey Brennan! Amy closed her eyes.

'Who is she?' Bob had momentarily forgotten the cold. 'She's very glamorous. Surely she doesn't drive one of those things?'

'Yes, she does.' Amy nodded. 'And she rides a huge motorbike to work. And she plays ladies' football.'

'Really?' Cicely brightened. 'She sounds interesting.'

'That's Jacey Brennan,' Amy said shortly. 'One of that huge family of Brennans that live on the other side of Appleford. You must know them – they're all as unruly as each other.'

'Unusual name,' Bob mused.

'Oh, she's got a proper name.' Amy sniffed. 'Josephine

4

Catherine. Shortened to Jacey – the initials. They're like that, the Brennans.'

Cicely gave her daughter-in-law a sharp glance.

'You don't approve, then?'

'Oh, goodness, Mum, you know what Mitchell's like. He's as wild as the wind. The last thing he needs is a girlfriend who considers herself one of the boys.'

'She doesn't look like one of the boys.' Bob whistled appreciatively, earning himself another glare from Amy and a shake of the head from his mother.

'Let's face it.' Cicely snuggled further into the warmth of her padded coat. 'Mitchell would never go for a meek and mild girl, would he? Not like Megan, say?'

'At least Megan behaves like a lady!' Amy protested.

'Considering she's a taxi driver?' Bob joked. 'And she may well behave more decorously than what's-her-name out there, but she's no more sensible in her love life, is she?'

'No.' Amy wouldn't be drawn. 'Oh, well, one day they'll all be married, like Matt, and then we won't have to worry.'

'Don't you believe it.' Cicely linked arms with her son and daughter-in-law. 'You never stop worrying. Still, Matt's done well with young Sally – and they've made me a great-grandmother. I can't see Megan doing that – not if she continues to hang around with Peter King.'

'He wouldn't be my choice either.' Amy stared at the track, trying not to watch Jacey Brennan holding on to Mitchell's arms as she laughed. 'But they practically grew up together. Peter and Megan are –'

'Like an old married couple!' Cicely snorted. 'No sparkle, no excitement, no nothing. He's boring.'

Luckily Amy was spared having to agree as the drivers all suddenly scrambled back into their disreputable vehicles. As always, she felt a frisson of excitement as the over-tuned engines roared into life and the cold, bleak afternoon was filled with the stench of hot oil.

There seemed no rhyme or reason to the start of the race.

The cars, jammed together like some multiple pile-up, quivered and snarled, the drivers firmly belted into their seats, waiting for the marshal's flag.

It was a nail-biting moment The air throbbed. The scream of the engines was intense. The flag dropped.

As the cars, obscured in a foul-smelling cloud of dust, roared towards the first bend, Amy's heart was in her mouth.

'And you tell me what you think I should be doing with my life!' Sally Phillips strode angrily towards the window and stared out across the windswept garden without seeing anything. 'Go on, Matt. Tell me.'

'For heaven's sake,' Matt laid his hands flat on the table, 'don't shout. Kimberley's only just gone off to sleep, and Gran and Granddad Foster will be able to hear every word.'

'Fine.' Sally turned back into the living room and faced her husband. 'Then they can report back to your mum and dad as soon as they return from the stock cars, can't they? It'll save you having to do it.'

'That's not fair, Sally.' Matt stood up. 'You make it sound as though I always run to Mum and Dad every time we have a row. I don't –'

'Which is just as well.' Sally glared. 'Because if you did, you'd never be away from them, would you? It's all we seem to do these days, row. And we're never on our own. Never!'

Matt sighed as he looked at her. Her hair was escaping from its knot on top of her head, her green eyes blazed, and he thought she looked lovely. But when had he stopped telling her? She was always so angry these days.

He held out his hand. 'Come and sit down, Sally. Come on – we'll talk about it.'

Sally didn't budge. 'That's all we ever do – talk. And nothing changes, does it, Matt? We live in our bit of this bungalow, with your parents on one side, your grandparents on the other, with Megan always in and out and Mitchell living in the loft conversion. I'm surrounded by your blasted

6

family morning, noon, and night!'

'Lavender Cabs is a family business …' Matt bit back his own rapidly rising temper. 'You knew that when you married me.'

'Sure I did. But I married you, Matt, not the other three hundred members of the Phillips clan! I want my own business, can't you understand? I want my own home. I don't want to live as part of the Phillips family empire, involved in taxis and hire cars and garages and mess and noise. I don't want to be surrounded by bits of cars, oily rags, and people ringing twenty-four hours a day to be taken to airports or theatres or restaurants! When did I last see any of those?'

'Yes, well, with Kim –'

Sally bit her lip, and her hands shook. She knew she would have to be careful.

'I love Kim, Matt, you know that. Desperately,' she said quietly. 'I couldn't bear to be without her. But you know as well as I do that an unplanned baby really didn't help things. I had dreams, and yes, I wanted a family, but not until my business got off the ground.

'And that's another thing,' she said quickly before he had time to argue. 'Your whole family dotes on Kim – which is lovely – but they spoil her rotten. There's always one or other of them picking her up, buying her things, pushing the buggy. I don't even have control over my own baby! That's why I want her to go to a childminder while I start this business. I need some freedom!'

'You don't need to go out to work, Matt pointed out.

'Oh, I do,' Sally said bitterly. 'I most certainly do.'

'Well, you don't need a childminder, then. Gran and Granddad Foster are only next door and Gran Phillips would –'

Sally almost stamped her foot. 'I am not leaving Kimberley with your family! Can't you see? That wouldn't help things at all. They'd treat her the way they want to and take no notice of what I said. I want her to grow up with the right values – not thinking that because she's a Phillips she can have everything she wants!'

Matt was finally roused to real anger.

'We're not like that!' he protested. 'We were never spoiled. We were loved and wanted, and once Mum and Dad were able to do it, they gave us things that mattered. That's what families are about. But of course you wouldn't know that, would you?'

The words were out before he could stop them, and when he looked at Sally's stricken face he was over-whelmed by remorse.

'Oh, Sally. I'm sorry. I didn't mean … Come here, love …'

'Go away! Don't come near me!' Sally's eyes had filled with tears and there was a tight knot burning her throat. 'How could you say that? How could you?'

Matt turned away, his shoulders slumping, unable to look at the pain in Sally's eyes.

Sally had no family. The only child of elderly parents, she had been orphaned at the age of ten, after which she had been brought up first in a children's home, and later by a succession of foster parents. He couldn't have hurt her more if he'd hit her.

'Sally …'

'Don't say anything.' Her lips were trembling. 'I am going to get a job, Matt, and not just a job. A career. I'm going to start my own aromatherapy business – away from the Phillipses, away from Lavender Cabs, away from this blasted homestead. Right away from Lavender Lane!

'And I'm not seeking your approval – I'm telling you what I'm going to do.'

'But isn't what you do with your oils and things now enough?'

'Oils and things!' Sally was still trying not to cry. 'They're not just oils and things, Matt! And running party plans in other people's houses is fine, but I've done the course and now I want to expand, to prove that I can do something myself!'

She marched past him and out into the tiny kitchen. Matt could hear her filling the kettle, angrily crashing cups around in the sink.

He felt drained – and bitterly ashamed of his outburst. How could he have been so insensitive?

When they had first met five years earlier, Sally had been delighted, if a little wary, at the thought of joining Matt's extended family. It was only after they had married and moved into their own self-contained part of the family bungalow that she had realised just how close the Phillips clan was.

Used to her independence, afraid of loving anyone too much, Sally resented the lack of privacy, the assumption that every Phillips had a right to know what all the rest were doing, and the fact that they were all bound, body and soul, to Lavender Cabs.

The only person who really understood her was Cicely, Matt's grandmother. Sally adored her, and Cicely secretly admired the fact that Sally obviously had far more gumption than Megan. They had soon formed an unholy alliance.

Matt got slowly to his feet and lounged in the kitchen doorway. Sally, her hair straggling around her neck, her face flushed with anger, didn't look at him.

'Sally, can we start that conversation again? I apologise for what I said. I wasn't thinking.'

'Do you ever?' She pushed past him and started stacking dishes in the sideboard. 'Matt, this is the first Saturday you've had off in months. Oh, I know the taxis were busy over Christmas and we needed the money – but you're not working today. And what do we do? Nothing!'

'What did you want to do? Watch Mitchell racing? Go to the rugby match with Megan and freeze to death watching Peter roll about in the mud?'

'No!' She clenched her fists. 'I didn't want to do anything

with the family. It's always the blasted family! Why couldn't we have gone out somewhere – just you, me, and Kim?'

'You didn't say –'

'And neither did you! I'm twenty-five, Matt, but I feel like I'm ninety! I want to live a little before I die –'

Suddenly Kimberley's wail echoed across the hall.

They glared at each other, then Matt moved away to comfort their daughter who had obviously been wakened by their raised voices.

'Don't pick her up,' Sally warned wearily. 'Just talk to her. She'll go off again.'

Matt sighed. 'I do know. She's my daughter, too.'

Sally slumped at the table. The afternoon was passing too quickly. The family would be back soon, and once again there would be no privacy.

She felt so trapped. If only Matt could understand. If only he could see further than Lavender Cabs!

The phone rang, and Sally stretched out a lethargic hand. It probably wouldn't be for her.

'Hello? Oh, hello, Judith. No, they're all out. Megan's at Peter's rugby match – the rest of them have gone stock car racing. Yes, all right, I'll tell her. Bye.'

'Who was that?' Matt emerged from the bedroom with Kim snuggled in his arms. 'And before you say anything, I didn't mean to pick her up. I just couldn't resist her ...'

Sally looked at him, and at their beautiful pink-and-white daughter in her cuddly sleep-suit, and smiled.

'I know. I never can either. Oh, Matt ... what's gone wrong with us?' she sighed.

'Nothing.' Relief swept over him at her change of mood. 'At least, nothing that can't be sorted. Look, why don't we ask Gran Foster to babysit for Kimberley and we'll go out for a meal? Would you like that?'

'Could we talk about the business?' she asked warily.

'Do we have to?' he ventured, but he caught sight of the

fresh fury dawning in her eyes and sighed. 'All right, if you must.' He bent his head to breathe in Kimberley's sweet baby smell. 'And who was that on the phone?'

'Aunt Judith.' Sally was smiling now. The whole evening alone with Matt – surely she would be able to persuade him to change his mind. 'She wants to see your mum – urgently.'

Matt groaned. 'Oh, no. Then we really will be better off out of the way tonight. I don't think I can stand another one of their showdowns. I bet Uncle Paul's at the back of it again.'

'Probably.' Taking Kim from Matt's arms, Sally tickled her until she gurgled. 'Still, it's one side of the Phillips power struggle that we don't have to be involved in, isn't it?'

'Er … yes,' Matt didn't meet her eyes. 'I suppose it is …'

Megan Phillips tapped her fingers against the steering-wheel. She would give Peter another five minutes. If he didn't turn up then, she was going home without him.

The wind buffeted the side of the car, and Megan shivered. Even with the heater on full, it would take ages to get warm again.

She had stood on the touchline for the full eighty minutes, watching Peter's team win handsomely, dutifully cheering every try, every conversion. Before that, she had been up to her armpits in the traditional team tea, helping the other wives and girlfriends prepare the gargantuan feast their menfolk expected.

A sharp rap on the window made her stop drumming her fingers. Neil James, one of Peter's cronies, was squinting in at her.

She wound down the window and shuddered in the icy blast.

'Peter says to tell you he's having one for the road. He wondered if you'd rather come in and join him.'

'Too right I would.' Megan scrambled from the car. 'If I don't, he'll stay in there for the duration, re-living every darned moment. Thanks, Neil. You off home?'

'Yes, he is.' Jenny, Neil's wife, was tugging at his arm and laughing. 'I've got my man under control, Megan. You ought to do the same with yours.'

The rugby club was crowded. The win had been spectacular, and the noisy good humour was even louder than usual.

Megan squeezed her way through the throng. She could see Peter, lounging against the bar, drink in one hand, gesticulating wildly with the other. Shaking her head, she shouldered her way towards him.

Peter King was Matt's best friend from school, three years older than her. Megan felt as though she had known him for ever. They had drifted into their easy-going relationship by sheer familiarity.

'Neil found you, then?' Peter, tall and thick-set with close-cropped dark curls, smiled. 'Shall I get you an orange juice?'

'Please.' Megan sighed. It was taken for granted that she would be the chauffeur on rugby match days so that Peter could either celebrate or drown his sorrows.

Sometimes, after driving a Lavender cab all week, Megan would have liked to leave the driving to someone else and indulge in a glass or two of wine. But she'd never voiced the wish, and as with everything else, Peter took it for granted that she was perfectly happy.

'Mr Bamford was out there today, watching.' Peter covered Megan's hand with his large one. 'That's one of the few times he's ever been to see us play.'

Mr Bamford was the manager of the bank where Peter and most of the team worked.

'He was probably making sure you're all still fit enough to turn up for work on Monday morning.' She grinned. 'He's probably more interested in safeguarding his staff than in assessing your skills in a scrum.'

Peter nodded philosophically. He never argued, never

really volunteered an opinion. He was placid and plodding, both in his work and with Megan.

'Jennifer was saying that Neil's applied for assistant manager in one of the Oxford branches.' Megan sipped her orange juice. 'Didn't you think of applying for it? After all, you and Neil have been at the Appleford branch for the same length of time.'

'No.' Peter shook his head and waved his empty glass across the bar for a refill. 'With all the reorganisation in banking, I'm quite happy to stay as a personal advisor for the time being. I've got my eye on old Bamford's job when they put him out to grass.'

'Surely they won't promote from within? They'll bring in someone who has at least been assistant manager somewhere, won't they?'

'Maybe.' Peter shrugged, draining an inch from the top of his fresh pint. 'Still, I'm quite happy to bide my time. Why rock the boat, eh?'

Why indeed, Megan thought wearily, catching sight of her reflection in the mirror behind the bar. She barely reached Peter's shoulder, and with her straight hair cut into a bob, and all her make-up whipped away by the biting wind, she looked like her mother.

Peter was suddenly swallowed up by a crowd of back-slapping cronies, and Megan found herself elbowed aside.

Irritably, she finished her drink and pushed her way back to him.

'I'm ready to go, Peter. You won't be long, will you?'

This was met by jeers and ribald remarks from Peter's friends, and she half-smiled.

'OK. So one of you will drive him home then, will you?'

'Come on, Megan.' One of his mates, Toby, put his arm round her shoulders. 'Loosen up a bit.'

'Yeah!' Another, Nigel, grinned. 'After all, a rugby man's wife has to know her place.'

'Really?' Megan's eyebrows arched above dangerously

glittering eyes. 'Then it's just as well that I'm not one, isn't it?'

'Ah, but it won't be long,' Toby persisted. 'We've told Pete – he's got to arrange his wedding outside the season. We can't afford to lose him on a Saturday ...'

'And who's the poor unfortunate girl?' Megan looked past Toby and Nigel to where Peter was laughing. 'Do I know her?'

They all laughed more loudly, and Megan suddenly found it extremely irritating.

'You mean he hasn't asked you yet?' Toby shook his head. 'Maybe he'll do it next Saturday night.'

'Why?' Megan asked. 'Why next Saturday night?'

'It's the dinner and dance.' Nigel shook his head at her forgetfulness.

'When even a rugby player's thoughts stray to love and romance. It's not just a disco and chicken and chips; we've got a sit-down meal and a proper band.'

'I know.' Megan was feeling tired now. 'But it'll still be an excuse for drinking and joking and your usual loud behaviour, won't it? I can't see it being a wine and roses occasion – after all, you can't make a silk purse out of a sow's ear, can you?'

Toby and Nigel looked shocked, and Peter frowned.

'That's a bit uncalled for, Meg. You've always enjoyed the dances ...'

'Have I?' Megan said, quietly but very clearly.

After all these years, he still didn't really know her. She had accompanied him to all manner of functions, not drinking so that she could drive him home, sitting tight-lipped as the jokes and behaviour became sillier.

He didn't know that she would really like to go out with him, alone, be wined and dined and wooed. But then, she thought sadly, it was just as much her fault as his. She had never told him.

14

'I suppose we ought to be going then.' Peter drained his glass and winked at Toby and Nigel. 'My taxi driver's got the meter ticking.'

Peter slid into the passenger seat and fiddled with his seat belt as Megan drove slowly out of the club's car park.

Finally he settled back in his seat and looked across at her.

'You were a bit sharp with Toby and Nigel. They were only joking.'

'I know.' Megan steered the car carefully into the stream of traffic. 'But I've heard those jokes so many times! What is it about men getting together that makes them all behave as though they've never left the playground?'

'Oh, come on.' Peter turned in his seat to stare at her. 'Where's your sense of humour? You've been a misery all afternoon – you'd better cheer up by tonight.'

Megan pulled a face. 'What's on tonight? Something else connected with the rugby club that just seems to have slipped my mind?'

'We're meeting Neil and Toby and Nigel in the Blue Boar.' He was smiling happily again. 'Like we always do.'

'Oh, yes. Like we always do,' Megan echoed, manoeuvring the car towards the High Street.

They would meet Neil and Toby and Nigel at half past eight – as they always did – and while the men propped up the bar and discussed the day's game yet again, she would sit with Jenny, Theresa, and Sara, and discuss nothing much.

'Why don't we go out on our own tonight?' She drew up at red traffic lights. 'Why don't we give the Blue Boar a miss? After all, you'll see them all at the bank on Monday – and you've been with them all afternoon. Why don't we do something different tonight? Like go to the cinema.'

'What?' Peter couldn't have been more shocked if she'd suggested belly dancing in the marketplace. 'But we always go to the Blue Boar on a Saturday night.'

'Yes, of course we do. Silly me.'

15

Peter missed the danger in her tone, and relaxed again.

'You were joking, weren't you?'

'Yes.' Megan pulled away from the lights, too weary to argue. 'I must have been joking.'

Outside Peter's flat she switched off the engine while he scrabbled around for his sports bag.

'Just time for a bit of shut-eye before you come and pick me up again.'

'No.' Megan stared straight ahead. 'I'm not driving tonight.'

'You're not? Why not?' Peter was half in and half out of the car, and looked over his shoulder in surprise.

'Because I drive all day every day for a living. For as long as I can remember, I've driven you about so that you can have a drink with your friends. I'm a taxi driver all day – I don't want to be an unpaid chauffeur by night.'

'But you've never said anything before.' Peter looked hurt. 'Why the sudden change of heart?'

'It's not sudden,' Megan snapped. 'Look, will you either get in or get out? I've been freezing all afternoon for you – it's like Siberia out there – and at least the car is warm.'

Peter got back in and looked at her in concern.

'Meg, are you ill? You're not usually this snappy. Look, I'm sorry if you've not been feeling too good and I've made you hang around … would you rather stay in tonight?'

Megan almost laughed. At last she'd got through to him!

She nodded. 'I'll phone for a take-away and borrow that DVD Mitchell's been raving about. Mum and Dad are bound to be out somewhere tonight. We'll have the place to ourselves … Well, apart from Gran and Granddad Foster, Matt and Sally and Kim, and Mitch – but at least they're all self-contained. What time will you come round?'

Peter was staring at her as though she'd gone mad.

'I didn't mean that *we'd* have a night in, Meg. I meant that if you're not feeling well, it might be better for you to have an early night, and I'll meet up with the lads at the Blue Boar on my own.'

Not knowing whether to laugh or cry, Megan found herself doing both.

'Forget it, Peter.' She swallowed. 'Just forget it. I'll have a night in tonight, alone, with the DVD. You go and enjoy yourself with the lads ...' Her voice was rising hysterically and she fought to calm it. 'Just don't expect to find me waiting for you next time you need a chauffeur!'

She leaned across and almost pushed him out of the car before revving it into the sort of snarling take-off that would have won Mitchell's approval and made her parents wince.

As she tore away from the flat, she was aware that he was staring after her, his eyes troubled and confused.

'Selfish, selfish so-and-so,' she muttered, slowing the car to a more reasonable pace. 'I've been taken for granted for too long, Peter King! It's about time things changed!'

Chapter Two
A Point Of Conflict

The stock car circuit was practically obliterated by a cloud of dust that even the biting wind failed to shift, and by thick plumes of exhaust fumes.

The raw noise of the engines was only fractionally louder than that of metal crunching on metal.

Bob Phillips looked on in shock, but Amy and Cicely were leaping up and down beside him, screaming Mitch to victory.

Mitchell had always been a problem; always the one to climb the tallest tree, to jump from rope swings into the fastest flowing section of the river, to crash motorbikes, to do anything that was a little bit more daring than anyone else.

Bob knew his own staid and careful nature made this wild son of his almost a stranger to him on occasions, but watching him out on the track, risking life and limb, filled him with glowing pride. Mitchell was doing something that he would never dare undertake in a million years.

'Have you heard from Judith?' Cicely shouted in Amy's ear as the cars sped away from them on another circuit. 'I met your mother at the WI last week and she said that you still weren't speaking.'

'We speak.' Amy pulled a face. 'But neither of us says what the other wants to hear. Sometimes it seems terrible to have such a rift with my own sister but Judith is –'

'Bossy, overbearing, and ruled by that bad-tempered husband of hers.' Cicely, who always called a spade a spade,

19

nodded fiercely. 'I don't know why she thinks they should be getting a piece of Lavender Cabs anyway.'

Amy laughed. 'Well, I suppose when Mum and Dad retired three years ago, Judith automatically assumed Lavender – and the garage – would be split between both of us. I know Paul expected that when he came out of the army, they'd just move in and take over the running of one or the other.'

'Why should they?' Cicely bristled. 'You helped out as soon as you left school, when your Judith wanted to go to secretarial college and not get her hands mucky. Then you put yourself through those evening classes, even while Matt and Megan were small, so that you could take over the accounts properly. And my Bob –' She cast a fond glance towards her son, waving his arms excitedly as Mitchell's car once more tore into view. 'Well, he's worked for your dad since he was sixteen. Lavender Cabs belongs to you and Bob, my dear. Not to Paul and Judith and those awful children of theirs – and I shall tell her so when I see her!'

'Oh, please don't,' Amy said quickly, knowing Cicely was more than capable of doing so. 'It would only make matters worse. Oh, look – Mitch is in the lead!'

'And only one more circuit to go!' Cicely whooped her grandson on with enthusiasm. 'Come on, Mitch! Show 'em a clean pair of heels!'

Bumping and barging, rocketing into the crash barriers and bouncing back, the tangle of cars roared past them again.

Amy realised she was gnawing her nails, and guiltily stuffed her hands into her pockets. Her dark hair, still untouched by grey, swung about her face, and her hazel eyes widened.

This was always the most nerve-racking part of the race, when the cars that were left intact were battling it out in fierce determination in the final stages.

'That young Brennan girl is still up there with them!' Bob shouted in her ear. 'She's got some guts, hasn't she?'

Amy nodded reluctantly. Jacey Brennan's car – like every car she drove – was painted pale pink with lilac stripes. Jacey Brennan did not believe in hiding her light under a bushel.

'Anyway –' Cicely returned to her former train of thought as soon as the cars had roared past. '– what do Judith and Paul think they could contribute to Lavender, or the garage for that matter, that you and the children can't?'

'Judith thinks – or rather, I suspect Paul tells Judith to think – that the whole set-up is hopelessly old-fashioned. His idea is to leave Lavender Cabs to me and Bob, while they take over the garage. The last idea I heard was to sell it off to one of the chains and make a sort of diner-cum-supermarket as well ...'

'Stupid fool!' Cicely sniffed. 'The whole appeal of the place is the personal service, just as it was when your dad ran it and his father before him. And what does Paul know about running a business anyway? Oh – look! This is it! Mitch is in the lead! He's going to win this one, Amy! He's going to win!'

Bob and Amy clutched each other as Mitch's car screeched round the final bend on two wheels.

Bob's mouth was dry and his heart was thumping uncomfortably fast. Amy wanted to close her eyes, but found herself willing Mitch on, silently mouthing his name.

The driver of a black and gold car, sensing this was his last chance, drew alongside Mitch with a reverberating crunch.

Sparks flew. The crowd screamed.

For a split second the two cars seemed glued together, then with a metallic screech they parted and, almost in slow motion, Mitchell's car veered across the track and hit the barrier broadside.

For a moment it looked as though he was going to be able to control the spin, but at the last moment the car lurched on to its side. Over and over it rolled, dust surrounding it, bouncing from one side of the track to the other.

The crowd were silent for a second, then the screams started.

Bob, holding Amy and Cicely helplessly against him, watched in horror as the marshals poured on to the track and raced towards Mitchell's car.

He was praying as the other cars slewed to a halt all across the track.

'We must get to him.' Amy was trying to tug herself away. 'Bob! Let me go!'

'You can't do anything!' Bob said fiercely, feeling sick as an ambulance siren wailed through the mayhem. 'Look, the marshals are almost there now – oh!' The pink and lilac car had hardly quivered to a halt when Jacey Brennan, tugging off her helmet, her long blonde hair whipped by the wind, and tears pouring down her face, fought her way through the track marshals and hurled herself on Mitchell's car.

'Is he hurt?' Amy grabbed at the arm of the nearest person. 'How is he?' It seemed as though she was swimming against a tide of people as everyone crowded on to the track. 'Please let me through! He's my son!'

'Amy, don't.' Bob tugged at her arm. 'Look, over here. They're bringing him across here to the ambulance.'

'There!' Cicely said, relief swamping her voice. 'He's walking. No bones broken, then. Oh, Amy, don't cry ...'

In the mayhem, the Phillipses elbowed their way through to the ambulance. Mitch, supported by a paramedic, and even more closely by Jacey Brennan, was shaking his head.

'I'm fine.' He grinned sheepishly at his parents. 'Honestly.' He tapped the helmet that Jacey was carrying. 'That stopped any sense being knocked into me. I'll probably be a bit stiff in the morning – and the car's a write-off ...'

'Blast the car!' Bob growled, fear making him angry. 'You've just scared your mother and grandmother half to death.'

'Are you all right?' Amy squeezed herself past Jacey.

22

'Honestly?'

'Honestly.' Mitchell smiled gently. 'Sorry if I frightened you.'

'You didn't.' Cicely grinned at her grandson. 'We're just annoyed that you didn't win. You had that race sewn up.'

'Mother!' Bob protested, but Mitchell laughed.

'I feel like that, too. Still, there's always next time,' he promised breezily, and Amy closed her eyes with dread.

'I think we should just get you along to the hospital for a check-up,' the paramedic said. 'The track doctor will have a quick look at you, but you might need an X-ray.'

'We'll come with you,' Amy said quickly. 'Then we can drive you home.'

'There's no need for that, Mrs Phillips,' Jacey Brennan said softly, taking her eyes from Mitchell for the first time. 'I can do that. There's no need for everyone to go.'

'He's my son.' Amy's voice rang out sharply. 'If anyone goes with him it'll be us – his family.'

'Mum.' Mitchell touched Amy's shoulder. 'I'm perfectly all right, and I'm overage. They won't need your permission for anything. I doubt if I'll even need a visit to hospital – but if I do, I think it'd be better if Jacey came with me. I've made a complete mess of our afternoon as it is.'

Cicely put her arm round Amy's shoulders.

'I think what he's trying to tell us is that the last thing he wants is the Phillips entourage creating a fuss in the casualty department as though he were a five-year-old who'd just fallen off his swing!'

Amy glared at her mother-in-law, but Cicely ignored that.

'And more to the point,' she went on, 'why should he want a host of old fogeys clamouring around him when this young lady is more than capable of seeing that he gets home safely?' She smiled at Jacey. 'You go with him, my dear, if necessary, and then bring him home.'

Cicely always went too far. Annoyed, Amy looked to Bob

for support, but seeing that none was forthcoming, she shrugged.

'Perhaps you're right. But you come straight home from the hospital, Mitchell. No gallivanting – even if they do say you're OK.'

'No, Mum.' Mitchell's eyes twinkled. 'There is one thing you could do for me, though.'

'Yes?' Amy's fear had subsided, but her anger hadn't. 'And what's that?'

'Could you just see if the car can be salvaged, and then ask Luke to put the remains on a trailer and get it back to Lavender Lane for me? I can work on it in the morning.'

'No problem,' Bob agreed at once, wanting to defuse the situation, and then he stood back as a man approached. 'This looks like the doctor.'

The doctor, already briefed by the first-aid team, seemed to Amy to be completely unconcerned.

'Right, then, let's just check you over. Up into the back of the ambulance with you.' He turned to Bob, Amy, and Cicely. 'I don't think you need to hang around. He looks revoltingly healthy to me. And you, my dear –' he beamed at Jacey '– you'd better come up and hold his hand.'

To Amy's fury, the ambulance doors closed firmly, but not before she had seen Jacey Brennan melt into her son's arms.

Bob knew Amy was angry but there wasn't a lot he could do about it.

'I'll go and speak to Luke about getting the wreck back home. You and Mum can wait for me in the car.'

Cicely took Amy's elbow and together they forced their way through the milling mass of people. With the last race ending so abruptly, the crowds were drifting away.

'I can't believe it,' Amy smouldered. 'That girl! She's only known him five minutes – how dare she worm her way in like that!'

'Amy, dear!' Cicely was laughing as they reached the car.

'Put yourself in their place. Suppose that was Bob and you years ago and I'd wanted to fuss around. Wouldn't you have thought that it was your place to be with him? It's the order of things, my dear.'

'Yes, well, maybe ...' Amy unlocked the car, and the two women dropped gratefully into its warmth. She was always disgruntled by Cicely's ability to see everyone's point of view – it made her seem such a grouse.

'But that was different,' she went on. 'Bob and I were in love, we knew we would spend the rest of our lives together. If anything had happened to him I would have gone crazy. Of course I would have wanted to be with him in those circumstances. But Mitchell and this Jacey Brennan – well, that's different.'

'Is it?' Cicely said carefully. 'Do you think so?'

'Of course!' Amy settled herself behind the steering-wheel. 'Mitch has had so many girlfriends – he never keeps them long enough for me to get to know their surnames most of the time. Why should Jacey Brennan be any different?' She turned and stared at her mother-in-law in the back seat. 'Surely you don't think –?'

'Why not?' Cicely asked gently.

'Because ...' Amy shook her head. 'Because I don't like her!'

'And if I hadn't liked you, my dear, Bob would still have married you.' Cicely smiled. 'Luckily I thought you were wonderful – the daughter I never had. But what you think won't come into it. If Mitchell decides Jacey Brennan is the one for him, I'm afraid you'll just have to accept it.'

Luckily, Bob arrived at that moment, but Amy's heart was heavy.

Unhappy with Megan's drifting relationship with Peter King, and concerned about the increasing friction she sensed in Matt and Sally's marriage, she simply couldn't face Mitch falling for someone she felt was so unsuitable.

'Luke's taking the remains of the car home,' Bob said as

he eased himself into the passenger seat. 'Everyone seems to think they'll run Mitch up to the A and E as a matter of course, but he'll be fine. So there's no need for the gloomy face.'

Amy sketched a small smile as she manoeuvred the car towards the exit.

Cicely leaned forward between them.

'She's not fretting about Mitchell's injuries, Bob. She's worried about his heart.'

He frowned. 'His heart? But he's as strong as an ox – and twice as foolhardy! Goodness, Amy, there's nothing wrong with his heart.'

'There is when he's thinking of giving it to Jacey Brennan.' Cicely's voice was mischievous.

'Oh, I see.' Bob settled back into his seat. 'Well, I don't think we should make any judgment yet, do you? She's obviously very fond of Mitch, and …'

Taking one look at Amy's stony expression, he decided to say no more, and the rest of the short journey back to Lavender Lane was conducted in silence.

'Oh, no!' Amy groaned, as she turned into the driveway. 'That's all I need today!'

Bob followed her eyes and his heart sank.

'Oh, it's Paul and Judith's car!' Cicely said, leaning forward to peer through the windscreen. 'I was going to ask you to take me home, Bob, but I think I've changed my mind. I want to give that pair a good talking-to!'

'No!' Bob and Amy cried in unison, then looked at each other, laughing.

'At least we still agree on some things,' Bob teased, hugging her to him, relieved to see her smiling again. 'Even if it is only that Mother should occasionally keep her mouth firmly closed!'

'Actually –' Cicely observed as she scrambled from the car, '– Paul and Judith look as though they're visiting your first-born. And you might be glad of one of my well-timed remarks one of these days!'

'Yes, we might at that.' Amy grinned at her, then shivered as the icy wind blasted across the drive. 'Still, if we're not going to have to suffer the terrible twosome, I think it calls for a celebratory cuppa, don't you?'

They hurried up the steps, anticipating the cosy surge from the central heating as Bob unlocked the front door.

Bringing up the rear, Cicely groaned.

'Cancel the celebration,' she muttered. 'You've been spotted. They're on their way over ...'

Chapter Three
'Why Won't You Listen to Me?'

Jim and Stella Foster sat in their grandson Matt's small sitting room and looked at each other in concern.

'Judith isn't going to give up, is she?' Stella bit her lip. 'Maybe we should have considered letting them into the business when you retired ...'

'No.' Her husband shook his head. 'I knew what I was doing then, and I do now. I don't want to fall out with Judith – heaven knows, she's our daughter – but these hare-brained ideas aren't hers, Stella. They're Paul's, and he's only interested in making money. He doesn't have any feeling for the garage or Lavender Cabs.

'No, Bob and Amy have been with us right from the start. They mucked in and went without when Paul and Judith were swanning round the world with the army and wouldn't have given a thank you for our business on a plate. It's too late now for them to want to become involved.'

'Poor Amy!' Stella shuddered. 'I'm sure all she wanted to do was get indoors and defrost her toes with a cup of tea in front of the fire. She doesn't want Judith nagging about how the garage could benefit from the injection of Paul's golden handshake.'

Jim stood up and walked to the window. It was growing dark, and the wind was chasing black clouds across a slate-grey sky.

He didn't feel he'd been unfair to his younger daughter, but he was very aware that outsiders might see it differently.

29

He knew better than anyone the love and effort that Amy and Bob had put into his business at a time when Judith and Paul had found Appleford and Lavender Cabs almost an embarrassment.

'I suppose Judith tried to blackmail you by talking about the kids?' Jim turned and looked at his wife. 'Paul did with me. He said it was hardly fair that three of our grandchildren should be involved in the business while Dean and Debbie went without.'

'I got much the same,' Stella admitted. 'I said it was rubbish. We've always treated Debbie and Dean the same as Matt, Megan, and Mitchell. We may not have seen them so often, or been involved in their lives because they've spent so long abroad, but they've never been loved less.' She sighed wearily. 'This is becoming a complete nightmare.'

'Never mind.' Jim plonked down on the sofa again. 'We've got the whole evening babysitting our great-granddaughter to look forward to – and if I'm not mistaken, I think I saw Cicely with Bob and Amy. She'll be able to cut Paul down to size!'

'You're a wicked old so-and-so!' Stella laughed. 'I wouldn't wish Bob's mum on my worst enemy when she's in the mood to speak her mind!'

'What are you two giggling about?' Matt wandered through from the bedroom, fastening his tie. 'Have I missed out on a joke?'

'No.' Stella was still smiling. 'Just the thought of Cicely giving her own special brand of homespun advice to your Uncle Paul and Aunt Judith!'

Matt didn't smile. His aunt and uncle's visit couldn't have come at a worse time. Sally was in such a good mood now, and so looking forward to their evening out; he didn't want Paul or Judith letting the cat out of the bag. No point in raising her hopes yet …

And he certainly didn't want to talk about his plans in front of Gran and Granddad Foster. It had taken all his powers of ingenuity to keep avoiding the very subject Paul and Judith so desperately wanted to discuss.

'Oh, they'll all be so full of Mitchell's race that Paul and Judith won't be able to get a word in!' he said lightly, hoping it was true. 'Then Megan will be in with a replay of Peter's rugby match. I'm sure they won't even get round to discussing their inheritance – or lack of it.'

'Do you think I was wrong, then?' Jim looked quickly at his grandson, catching something in Matt's voice. 'Do you think I should have split the business between them and your parents?'

'No – no, of course not,' Matt said hastily. 'I didn't mean that. It was entirely up to you, and anyway, it's been Mum and Dad's life for ever. Er – I'd better go and see if Sally's anywhere near ready, otherwise we won't make the restaurant in time.'

Once he'd gone, Stella glanced at her husband.

'Why did you ask him that? You don't think –?'

He shrugged. 'I just had a feeling that there's more going on between young Matt and our Judith than meets the eye. I wouldn't like to think they're up to something – not something that would affect the business.'

'Not Matt.' Stella shook her head. 'Our grandson has Lavender Cabs running through him like his life's blood. He'd be as miffed as the rest of us if Paul got his way and sold the garage off to one of these modern setups.'

'Which is why, as long as I'm still alive,' Jim said firmly, 'neither Judith nor Paul will get their hands on the business.'

Just then Matt and Sally came into the room, Sally carrying Kim, gurgling happily in her arms.

'You look lovely, my dear,' Stella said, standing up to take her great-granddaughter into her arms. 'Are you going somewhere nice?'

'The new Italian in Oxford,' Matt put in. 'But we could only get an early table –'

'– so we thought we'd make the most of it and get in to the late showing at the cinema afterwards – if that's all right,'

31

Sally finished, looking anxiously at Stella and Jim. She was so looking forward to an evening out. She didn't want them to say they couldn't babysit after nine o'clock or something awful. 'You didn't want us home early, did you?'

'Definitely not.' Jim was tickling Kim's toes. 'You stay out as long as possible – we don't get to spend much time with this little lady.'

Feeling young and free again, Sally linked her fingers through Matt's as they hurried out into the dark, cold evening.

'Paul and Judith are still in with your mum and dad,' she said as Matt opened the car door for her. 'Did they say much to you while I was in the bath?'

'Not a lot. The usual stuff. They still want a share of the business.'

'There's not a chance of that,' Sally said, snuggling happily into her seat as the car purred off in the direction of Oxford. 'Is there?'

'Probably not.' Matt was concentrating on the traffic. 'Lavender Cabs is firmly entrenched in the past. Paul's subversive plans will frighten them all to death.'

Sally peered through the darkness, trying to see his face. There was something in his tone she didn't quite understand.

However, Lavender Cabs and the Phillips family was not what she wanted to talk about tonight so she decided to let it drop.

It wasn't until they were seated at their table, with the starters in front of them, that she took a deep breath and broached the subject that was uppermost in her mind.

'Matt – about my aromatherapy …'

'What about it?'

'I've worked out a business plan. I want to see the bank manager – Mr Bamford, Peter King's boss. I want to know if it's viable.'

'We haven't got the money to back it,' he protested.

'I could get a business loan. There's that little shop in the High Street that's been empty for ages. I could combine the oils with herbal remedies and health foods and that sort of thing ...'

Matt leaned across the table, gazing intently at her.

'Sally, we simply don't have the money! Look, can't you carry on doing house-to-house and party stuff for a little bit longer?'

'No.' Sally smiled. 'Anyway, we do have some money, don't we?'

'Not enough. And what happens if you have another baby?'

'I won't,' she said firmly, and he scowled.

'You mean you don't want to. You mean that this aromatherapy thing is more important than giving Kimberley a brother or sister?'

'Actually, yes, at the moment,' she told him, and sighed. 'Matt – don't let's fight over this. You're doing what you want with your life – please let me do the same. At least you're happy with Lavender Cabs ...'

He reached over and squeezed her hand.

'I want you to be happy, Sally. I know how important all this is to you. It's just that we don't own our own home, I'm not paid a vast amount, we've got virtually no savings – all in all, I don't think Mr Bamford – or any other bank manager – will welcome you with open arms.'

'Couldn't we borrow the money?'

'No!' Matt drew back. 'We can't get into debt now. And certainly not for –'

'Not for my silly idea of aromatherapy?' Sally's voice was sharp with anger. 'But no doubt if Megan wanted to set up a seal sanctuary or Mitchell wanted to teach senior citizens to hang-glide, that would be a different matter! Family first – and me second! That's it, Matt, isn't it?'

'No, actually, it isn't.' Matt's voice was low, but his anger showed. 'You and Kim are more important to me than anything. I've been doing a lot of thinking, too. I'm prepared to help you all I can ... but not just yet. Please be patient, Sally. I've got plans.'

'Plans to buy a new taxi? Plans that don't have anything at all to do with what I want!'

'Stop being so selfish!' Matt snapped. 'An aromatherapy business will hardly make us a fortune, will it? It might make a steady income, but it won't be enough to keep the three of us. We need something more, something I'm working on.'

'What?'

'I've already told you too much.' He was grinning again. 'Now, no more discussions about the business, your aromatherapy, or anything else. Tonight we're going to recapture our youth!'

'We're hardly in our dotage,' Sally protested as she polished off her melon and grinned back.

'No, but as you reminded me earlier, we were beginning to behave like it. What with Megan and Peter acting like Darby and Joan, we were in danger of becoming exactly like them.'

Sally was intrigued. Matt seemed to have had a complete change of heart ever since Judith and Paul's visit. She wished she knew more about what was happening.

Then she smiled to herself. She'd ask Cicely tomorrow when she called round for coffee. After all, she and Cicely had plans of their own ...

All the following week, Megan kept looking in at the jars and packages hidden in the top drawer of her dressing table.

Peter, obviously miffed at her sticking to her guns the previous Saturday, hadn't been in touch, and Megan was determined that she wouldn't be the one to make the first move.

Otherwise, life in Lavender Lane seemed to be running

fairly smoothly.

Mitch, bruised but otherwise unhurt, was back at work, vowing to take part in the next weekend's race come hell or high water. Matt and Sally seemed happy, and Aunt Judith and Uncle Paul had stayed away from her parents since the night of Mitch's accident.

Megan spent the week counting the days until Saturday, when she could put her careful plan into action, but at last it arrived, and as she handed over her taxi to the night driver and hurried home, she was relieved to see no sign of her parents or Mitchell. She needed the house to be empty. Any interruption, however well-meant, would only interfere with her plans.

She noticed that, once again, Paul and Judith's car was parked outside Matt's part of the house and Megan gave a wry grin. She certainly didn't envy Matt and Sally their visitors!

Her own bed-sitting room at the rear of the bungalow gave her privacy, and she was locked in her tiny bathroom when she heard the rest of her family return from the race meeting.

She'd go in and see them later. Right now, she had something far more important to do!

She heard her parents' voices raised, and Cicely's laughter, followed by a tapping on the front door. She turned off the shower and listened.

Paul and Judith! Megan smiled again. They weren't going to give up.

She wrapped a towel round her dripping hair and disappeared into the bedroom in search of the hairdryer.

Ten minutes later she surveyed the result. Her dark hair now gleamed a deep burgundy. It was an improvement, but not the dramatic difference she had wanted. Maybe if she applied the new make-up ...

Ten minutes later she looked at herself again. Now her eyes glowed dark and lustrous, her lips were a soft pink, and the dusting of blusher accentuated her cheekbones.

She nodded at her reflection, pleased with the result. At least she was doing this for herself – not for Peter.

If she ever saw Peter again, he probably wouldn't notice if she had become ash blonde and wore three pairs of false eyelashes – just as long as she was there to help with the rugby teas, bolster his ego, and drive him around!

Half an hour later, dressed in jeans, boots, and a thick black sweater, she tiptoed across the hallway to Bob and Amy's sitting room door.

What would her parents think of the transformation?

At least Cicely would approve, she knew that. Gran had always refused to grow old gracefully, and still dyed her hair to suit her mood – or sometimes even her outfit.

Megan paused before opening the door. She could hear Aunt Judith's strident voice, and winced. There was no way she could face going in there with another family argument in full swing.

'I think Mum and Dad should have given shares to Dean and Debbie when they reached eighteen. After all, all yours got them, didn't they?'

'On the understanding that they would be involved in Lavender Cabs,' Megan heard her father answer angrily. 'Mitchell didn't want to be, so his shares reverted to Mum and Dad Foster. Really, Judith, don't you think that –'

'I think that Dean and Debbie have been treated very shabbily. Debbie could have worked with you, Amy, in the front office, and Dean could have been employed in the garage instead of you taking on that Luke Dolan.'

'Now hold on, Judith –'

Megan grinned as she heard Cicely's voice. She would give them what-for!

'Debbie behind the desk would frighten away the customers, with those earrings and nose studs and a haircut that makes her look like an angry chicken. As for Dean – well, he knows absolutely nothing about cars or mechanical things, does he? He's a very clever musician. He wants to study the piano. What the devil would he want with an apprenticeship in a garage?'

'That's beside the point …' Uncle Paul entered the fray.

Megan sighed. It looked as if the argument would run round in the usual circles for ages yet. She would come back when the coast was clear. In the meantime, she'd ask Mitchell what he thought of her new image …

But his flat in the loft conversion was empty, and Megan was suddenly swamped with loneliness.

It was Saturday night, and everyone was doing something except her. She leaned her elbows on the windowsill and saw the light in the garage.

Of course! Mitchell would be down there working on his car. She'd go and share a cup of coffee with him, listen to his stories about the stock car meeting and cry on his shoulder about Peter's insensitivity.

Shivering in the biting wind, she pulled the garage door open and slipped inside. Music blared from the radio, there was a smell of coffee mingling with the stench of oil and petrol, and Mitchell's stock car looked like it had been through a crushing machine.

'Good heavens!' Megan said to the apparently empty garage. 'What happened, Mitchell?'

There was no reply. Megan switched off the radio, and immediately a pair of oil-stained jeans emerged from beneath the car. She grinned.

'I thought that would fetch you out. What on earth happened to the car – oh!' Her eyes widened. 'Oh, hi, Luke. I – er – thought you were Mitchell.'

'And I thought you were Megan.' Luke Dolan, Lavender's mechanic and Mitchell's friend, straightened up and grinned as he cast his eye appraisingly over her, taking in the burgundy hair that softly framed her face, the subtle make-up, the soft sweater, and shook his head. 'It's quite a refurbishment.'

'Oh!' Megan blushed. 'Do – um – you like it?'

'Very much.' He wiped his hands on a rag. 'But then, I was pretty keen on the original, too ... Would you like some coffee?'

'I'd love one, but I don't want to interrupt you. Where's Mitchell?'

'Being kissed better by Jacey Brennan.' Luke laughed, splashing water into the kettle. 'He came a real purler again this afternoon – hence my overtime, it wasn't as bad as last week's though, he actually managed to win this one. Didn't your mum and dad tell you?'

Megan shook her head, feeling guilty.

'Was he hurt again?'

'Not at all. He and Jacey are out celebrating, and as I didn't have anything planned for this evening I said I'd give the car the once-over. What about you, Meg – are you going somewhere special tonight? You look really fantastic.'

'Nowhere. I just felt like changing my image.'

She watched Luke rinsing out two mugs and setting out milk and sugar on a tray in her honour.

He was the same age as Mitchell, three years her junior, and she had always treated him with easy familiarity, like an honorary younger brother. His hair gleamed under the strip lights, and his blue eyes crinkled as he stirred the coffees.

'Where's Peter tonight?' he said as he handed her one of the mugs. 'I thought you and he were inseparable on Saturdays?'

'We were.' The scalding coffee burned her lips. 'That was something else I felt like changing. Oh, not permanently – just for a little while. Last week I couldn't face the Blue Boar.'

'Blue Boring, more like!' Luke grinned. 'But then, that suits Peter ... Oh, sorry. I shouldn't have said that.'

'No, you shouldn't.' Megan smiled back at him despite

herself. 'Anyway, Peter must have taken umbrage, because I haven't heard from him since. And why aren't you out setting the town alight tonight?' she teased him. 'I thought there were hordes of girls hanging round you and Mitchell, on the stock car circuit.'

'Millions,' Luke agreed with a laugh as he sipped his coffee. 'But then, I'm pretty choosy. And I've got my eye on someone special.'

'Oh.' For some unaccountable reason, her heart sank. 'Anyone I know?'

'She's older than me – and attached.' Luke shrugged. 'So I have to love from afar.'

'Dangerous ground.' Megan placed her coffee mug on the tray, not looking at him. 'She's not married?'

'No. I'm not that stupid.'

It was the silence that made her raise her head. Luke was staring at her. Suddenly her mouth went dry and a blush rose to her face.

Luke placed his mug beside hers on the tray and leaned towards her across the oil-smudged work bench.

'Peter King doesn't deserve you,' he murmured, but whatever she was going to say to that was wiped from her mind because when Luke Dolan kissed her the world tumbled upside down.

'Megan!' Cicely's voice rang through the garage. 'Meg! Are you in here?'

Guiltily Megan leapt away from Luke, her heart still racing.

'Over here, Gran.' Her voice sounded high-pitched and breathless.

'I've been sent to search for you.' Cicely bustled round the work bench and stopped short. 'Well, well!'

'Good evening, Mrs Phillips.' Luke seemed as flustered as Megan. 'I – er – we didn't hear you come in.'

'Obviously not.' Cicely was beaming at them both.

'Maybe I should have knocked. Heavens above, Megan – you look gorgeous!'

'Pardon?' Megan, her senses still reeling, stared at her grandmother.

'Your hair, my dear. And your make-up. Not, of course, to mention that rather becoming flush in your cheeks and the twinkle in your eye.'

'Gran!'

'Actually, you hardly seem dressed for the occasion.' Cicely was still beaming. 'But I don't suppose it'll matter.'

'What occasion?' Megan stared blankly .

'The rugby club dinner and dance? At least, I assume that's what Peter has come to collect you for.'

Megan clapped her hand to her mouth. 'Oh! I'd completely forgotten.' Then she scowled. 'He's got a nerve! I haven't even spoken to him all week. How dare he just turn up here assuming –'

'You'd better go and see him, Meg.' Luke picked up his spanners again. 'He's probably holding out an olive branch.'

Megan snorted and Cicely shook her head.

'He's actually holding a bunch of rather fine long-stemmed roses, but I think it is a peace offering. So unless you intend going to the dinner and dance dressed in jeans, Megan, I think you should skedaddle back to the bungalow ...'

'I don't intend going to the dinner and dance at all!'

'Of course you do.' Cicely looked at her. 'Get a move on or you'll have Peter in here looking for you – and I don't think that would be such a good idea, do you?'

Glaring at her grandmother and with a beseeching glance at Luke, Megan hurried from the garage.

Cicely waited until the door had closed and then smiled gently at Luke.

'It'll be all right. She just needs to work things out in her own way, and refusing to go with Peter tonight won't help things at all. Believe me, I know what I'm talking about.'

'I – didn't mean to kiss her,' Luke admitted. 'I just suddenly wanted to – very much.'

I'm sure you did, and she obviously enjoyed it. It's about time someone kissed Megan properly.' Cicely tapped his arm. 'And don't you worry about Peter King.'

Luke moved back to Mitchell's car and shook his head.

'I shouldn't have done it. Megan and Peter have been together for years – and I'm so much younger than she is. I don't think it'll happen again,' he concluded rather sadly.

Cicely sighed, but, wisely, for once said nothing.

Back in her room, Megan hurriedly shrugged on her black jersey dress and a pair of high-heeled black shoes. She had no time to sort out her feelings about Luke's kiss.

However, when she stormed into her parents' sitting room, she was furious at Peter's assumption that he could just turn up tonight and expect her to be ready.

Bob and Amy were making brave attempts to entertain him. Their eyebrows rose at their daughter's transformation, but before they could say anything, Peter had risen to his feet.

'Megan! You look nice.'

Nice! She fumed inwardly. Trust Peter to use such a bland word about her appearance!

'You've got a cheek!' She accepted the roses that he pushed towards her.

'Um – thank you … But you have, Peter – you've got a nerve just turning up here like this!'

'But you knew the do was tonight.' Peter looked at Bob and Amy for support but they kept their eyes downcast. 'I thought you'd have had a cooling-off period, and –'

'Cooling-off period!' Megan glared at him. 'There was nothing to cool off!'

Her dad coughed.

'Er – Megan. I think that if you and Peter intend going out, you should perhaps carry on this discussion on the

41

journey, don't you?'

Still fuming, Megan nodded and turned to Peter, who was smiling.

'Are we taking your car?' she asked.

'No.' He linked his arm through hers. 'And we're not taking yours, either. I've just arranged with your mum and dad for a taxi. That way we can both have a drink and –'

'There's no one free,' she protested. 'It's Saturday night. We're always booked solid.'

'Luke's in the garage, isn't he?' Bob asked. 'He can drive you. I'll pay him extra …'

'No!' Megan snapped, and they all stared at her. 'I mean – Luke's really busy with Mitchell's car. I popped in there earlier and – er –' She knew she was blushing. She swallowed. 'I don't mind driving.'

'But I thought you wouldn't want to drive.' Peter's brow was furrowed. 'I thought –'

'Tonight I feel like driving. And we've got a lot to talk about – all of which will be better said in private.'

Shrugging, Peter allowed Megan to drag him from the room.

Bob stretched his feet out in front of the fire and glanced at his wife. 'And just what was all that about?'

'I'm not sure.' Amy was still shell-shocked from her sister and brother-in-law's visit. She was hardly in any mood to cope with the undulations in Megan and Peter's romance. 'You could have knocked me down with a feather when Peter turned up – I'm sure Megan hasn't spoken to him this week.' She sighed, and then asked suddenly, 'Bob, how are we fixed financially?'

'How do you mean?' He had just lifted his newspaper, but he let it fall again. 'We're not on the verge of bankruptcy, if that's what you mean, but like all small businesses, we've known better days. Why?'

Amy looked wearily at him. 'Because right at this moment I would like to jump on a plane – even though I hate flying – and get as far away from Lavender Lane, Appleford, taxis, garages, stock cars – and, yes, the family – as possible. I really could do with a holiday.'

'Devon's pretty nippy at this time of year.' Bob laughed across the warm expanse of the hearth rug. 'And you don't need to fly there.'

'I don't mean Devon. I mean somewhere where we've never been before. Where all this carping and back-biting and tension can't touch us for a while. Somewhere where Paul and Judith can't keep barging in and playing for sympathy – where I don't have to watch Mitchell and Jacey Brennan smooching all over each other, or Megan and Peter rowing, or Matt and Sally trying to score points off each other all the time –'

'Hey, hey!' Bob leaned forward. 'Calm down, love. I had no idea it had got to you so badly. Look, I'm sure we could afford a break if you think it'll help. Matt could run the garage, Megan will be fine in the office – the drivers aren't a problem, and Mitchell and Luke do a darned good job …

But –' he took her hands in his '– the problems would still be here when we got back. Don't you think it would be better to sort things out before we went away? I don't mean about the kids – they'll have to make their own mistakes, like we did – and as long as we're around to pick up the pieces, we can't interfere. But as for your sister and that unspeakable husband of hers –!' His eyes flashed.

'I know.' Amy returned his comforting squeeze. 'I'm really thinking of asking Mum and Dad if they could be included in the business somehow just to make life easier …'

'No!' Bob was vehement. 'Over my dead body! Neither Paul nor Judith – nor those children of theirs – deserve a meal ticket at our expense. Don't even think about it!'

Amy leaned her head back and closed her eyes. Throughout their marriage, Bob had been the solid, dependable rock. Whatever horrors had arisen, he had coped with them in his calm, capable way, and their marriage had been all the stronger for it. But now …

She sighed. This awful bitterness between Judith and herself was something Bob had no control over.

Before long, she and her sister would have to have a meeting with their parents and thrash this thing out once and for all.

She groaned at the thought and Bob grimaced in sympathy.

'Amy …' He came to sit beside her, speaking as though he could read her mind. 'What's really troubling you? Surely it's not Paul and Judith? They've been singing the same song for ages, they'll soon get tired of it. And the kids are fine.'

'I don't think they are.' She opened her eyes again. 'Megan's far from fine she certainly shouldn't be thinking of marrying Peter just because they've always been together.

'Mitchell –' She shrugged. 'Well, Mitchell and that Brennan girl seem to be joined at the hip.

'Even Matt and Sally are like angry cats most of the time these days. I sometimes wonder if we did the right thing in providing them with all this.'

'We didn't have much choice,' Bob commented, settling back in his chair and watching the flames leaping up the chimney. 'We needed them to come into the business – and we had the space here to provide them with homes. You don't think we should have cast them out to struggle on their own, do you?'

'I'm beginning to think maybe we should have. And I know your mother thinks they're all mollycoddled.'

'Oh, Mother!' Bob laughed. 'She's an old reprobate! For goodness' sake, Amy, if she was a youngster now she'd probably be a New Age Traveller or something – just to shock people! No, I think we should just count our blessings. We've got each other, a nice little business, a home, and three children who are making their way in the world. Most people would be contented with a lot less.'

44

Amy knew he was right, and it certainly wasn't discontentment that she felt. But even in the cosy glow of the lamplight and with the log fire crackling comfortingly, she couldn't help feeling uneasy.

There was a little doubt niggling away in the back of her mind, a little doubt that was growing bigger by the minute. Somehow she sensed the family's cosy life was about to be rocked on its foundations.

Chapter Four
Our Secret

Having left Luke in the garage, Cicely Phillips shivered inside her sheepskin coat. She ought to call back in on Bob and Amy to tell them she was going home. She felt they really needed some time on their own, and although she welcomed the fact that they included her in their family life, there were times when she found it hard to bite her tongue.

For instance, if it was up to her, Judith and her family would be sent packing with a few home truths, and she was dying to be the one to do it.

And Mitchell should be allowed to see Jacey Brennan if he wanted to. Jacey was maybe a little unconventional, but Cicely really couldn't see why Amy should object to her so much.

As for Matt and Sally … Cicely's frown softened and she hurried along to tap on their door.

Sally, her hair escaping prettily from its confines as usual, smiled when she pulled it open and saw her visitor.

'Gran! I wasn't expecting you this evening! I thought you were having tea with Bob and Amy and then shooting off to one of your wild evenings.'

Cicely grinned as she stepped inside.

'Bessie Archer's Saturday night bridge parties cannot be described as wild! And anyway, I thought I'd spend some time with my favourite granddaughter – if that's all right.'

'Wonderful!' Sally assured her as she led her through to the sitting room. 'But I wouldn't let Megan hear you call me that!'

'Ah, yes – Megan.' Cicely's eyes twinkled. 'You'll never guess what she's been up to.'

She scooped Kim's toys off the sofa onto another chair and settled herself beside the gas fire, gratefully accepting the glass of sherry which Sally proffered.

'Is the coast clear?' she asked. 'I mean, we can gossip, can't we? Where's Matt?'

'Bathing Kim.' Sally sat opposite her. 'He can't hear us. What's all this about?'

'Well –' Cicely took a deep breath and proceeded to tell Sally all about Megan's transformation, Peter's unexpected arrival for the dinner and dance, and the fact that she had found Megan and Luke together, looking somewhat flustered.

'Really?' Sally's green eyes danced delightedly. 'Oh, good for Meg! She's always been so straitlaced – and Luke Dolan is gorgeous! I don't blame her! Not that I'd swap Matt for him, of course, but given the choice between Peter King and Luke Dolan – well …'

'Exactly!' Cicely nodded. 'Of course, Meg went off to her do – I told Luke that she had to. She has to finish with Peter first. I wonder what Bob and Amy will make of it?'

Sally considered just how her parents-in-law would react.

'Dad'll probably be shocked,' she concluded. 'I'd think Mum will be pleased, in the end. I wonder what made her change her hair and slap on make-up though? I mean, Megan never usually bothers about that sort of thing … '

'I'd like to think she did it for herself – but whatever the reason, it's a vast improvement.' Cicely commented. 'And what are you laughing at?'

'Nothing.' Sally giggled. 'I was just thinking – it makes a change for me and Matt to be the only Phillips children toeing the party line for once!'

'Well, that won't be for long, will it?' Cicely glanced towards the bathroom door. 'Have you mentioned anything to Matt yet?'

48

'I've dropped massive hints – but every time I think I've picked the right moment to discuss the business, he changes the subject. He keeps telling me to be patient – that he's got plans of his own.'

Cicely shook her head. 'Well, they certainly needn't involve buying that shop in the High Street, because I've signed the lease. You should be able to start decorating next month.'

Sally leaned across and hugged her. 'You know how grateful I am. As soon as we're up and running I'll start paying you back. I'll never be able to thank you enough, Gran. It was so important for me to have my own business. I want to prove that there is life in Appleford outside Lavender Cabs!'

Cicely returned her hug warmly. 'I'm really looking forward to it. It'll give me a whole new lease of life. And after all, all that money was just sitting in the building society. We'll be a wonderful partnership, Sally, dear, you dealing with the aromatherapy side of things and me with my flower and herb remedies. I've got all of my mother's recipes still – I can't wait to try them out.'

Sally laughed. 'You'll be a living ad! You've never had a day's illness in your life, have you?'

'Not that I can remember!' Cicely agreed. 'Since I was a child there's always been a remedy for everything. All my sniffles and aches and pains were nipped in the bud by a quick dose of something that smelled evil, but tasted like nectar.'

They giggled together and raised their glasses to their – so far – secret alliance. Sally just wished she had been able to tell Matt. She knew he would explode when he heard that Sally's Floral Oils was already a reality.

'And you won't have to worry about a childminder for Kim, will you?' Cicely continued. 'We'll just have her in the shop with us. There's a lovely little room at the back and that enclosed garden – it really couldn't be better.'

They smiled at each other again, then jumped guiltily as

the door opened.

'Where's Kimberley?' Sally looked at Matt in alarm. 'You haven't left her in the bath, have you?'

'Don't be silly! She's bouncing around in her cot. Oh, hi, Gran, I didn't hear you come in.'

Cicely smiled, then, carefully placing her sherry glass amidst Kim's building bricks and fluffy toys, she stood up.

'Why don't you two have a nice chat while I go and coo over my great-granddaughter? After all, you've done all the hard work.'

Once she'd disappeared from the room, Matt sat in the place Cicely had just vacated.

'Is Gran here for any special reason?'

'She just popped in for a chat before heading off to her bridge party.' Sally wasn't going to tell him about Megan, not yet. She'd save it for later, to soften the blow of her announcement and make him laugh. 'And a glass or two of sherry and a cuddle with Kimberley, of course.'

'Of course.' Matt stretched his legs out in front of the fire. He felt warm and contented. The wind was howling outside, and there was a possibility of snow forecast, but he was safe and snug with the two people he loved most in the world.

'Sally – when Gran's gone, we ought to talk.'

'What's wrong with now? There's a good film on later – and I've actually timed supper right so that we can eat it on our knees in front of the telly while we watch it.'

'Hmm – what I've got to say might cause you a bit of indigestion,' he said on a warning note, and she raised her eyebrows.

'Really?' Much as she loved Matt, she had to admit he wasn't noted for his sense of humour. Mitch seemed to have inherited both his brother's and his sister's share of fun. 'Well, shoot, then.'

He glanced towards the closed door. He didn't really want Cicely overhearing what he had to say. Well-meaning she might be, but he knew his grandmother was hardly the soul of discretion.

He lowered his voice. 'It's about your aromatherapy business.'

'What about it?' Despite the heat from the fire, Sally suddenly went cold. Surely Matt couldn't have heard that Cicely had bought that empty shop? 'You're not going to try to talk me out of it again, are you?'

'Far from it.' Matt smiled. 'I think I've got the answer.'

'Oh?' Sally was pretty sure she didn't want to hear what was coming next. 'And what's that? That I should forget all about it until Kim's old enough to go to school?' She shook her head. 'If that's what you want to tell me, Matt, then don't. I've said it a million times – I want to bring money into this house that has nothing to do with Lavender Cabs or Lavender Lane Garage or –'

'Sally, will you shut up for a minutes and listen to me?' He was laughing as he caught hold of her hands. 'I said I had the answer – and I have. I've sold my shares in Lavender to Paul and Judith.'

The Appleford Rugby Club Dinner and Dance was in full swing by the time Megan and Peter arrived.

'You're late,' Peter's friend Toby said, indicating their places at the table. 'We didn't think you were coming. But – wow!'

'What?' Peter remembered to hold out Megan's chair, and she gave him a small smile. 'Wow what?'

'Megan!' Toby leaned towards her. 'You look absolutely gorgeous. Good enough to eat. If that's what delayed Peter then it was well worth waiting for!'

'It wasn't,' Megan said shortly. 'What delayed him, I mean. But thank you, anyway.'

The first course was served almost immediately, and Megan concentrated on pushing her prawns around the dish. She couldn't eat.

The drive had been awful. Peter had been profusely

apologetic, she'd been offhand, and they had made most of the journey in silence.

Her heart still thundered at the memory of Luke's kiss. She had always thought he was attractive, but never in her wildest dreams had she imagined that he felt anything for her.

And now Peter was being the epitome of the loving boyfriend! Megan speared a prawn and groaned.

Jacey had been watching them and she leaned towards Mitchell with an amused grin.

'Your sister looks like she'd rather be anywhere else but here!'

'We're hardly rugby club material ourselves, are we? And Megan wasn't to know that your brothers let us have their tickets at the last moment …'

Jacey stared at him with amusement.

'Don't you talk to each other? In our family we all talk non-stop.'

'I've noticed.' Mitch laughed, managing to stroke Jacey's bare shoulder and eat at the same time. 'Yeah, we do normally. But Meg's been distracted this week – I think she'd had a fall-out with Mr King there. She's been doing all the extra shifts she could. We haven't seen each other much.'

'Even though you all live in the same bungalow?'

'Mum and Dad made sure we all had our own apartments as soon as we wanted them. We don't have to see each other if we don't want to.'

'It sounds perfect,' Jacey sighed, thinking of her own small home where her parents and five brothers and sisters all crammed together in noisy, happy harmony.

Mitch laid down his fork and looked at her. She was simply the most beautiful girl in the room, with her deep blue dress accentuating the sapphire of her eyes.

He wished his parents would see the good side of Jacey, instead of dwelling on her wild and crazy antics …

Halfway through the main course Peter leaned across the

table to Megan.

'Isn't that Mitchell down there?' he indicated. 'With Jacey Brennan?' Megan peered across the crowded room and exclaimed.

'Heavens! It certainly looks like it. I wonder how they got tickets? I wouldn't have thought this was their kind of thing.'

Peter smiled. It was the first time this evening that Megan had made any attempt at normal conversation.

'Meg …' Tentatively he touched her hand but she jerked it away and tried to concentrate on the roast beef in front of her.

'Sorry,' he muttered, looking miserable, then went on, 'Meg, we've got to sort things out. Look, I know I've been pig-headed and taken you for granted – but I've really missed you this week.'

'Have you?' Giving up the pretence at eating her meal, she laid her knife and fork together. 'Why?'

He blinked. 'Why? Well, because we've always been together, ever since school. Oh, I know we've had quarrels in the past – but this week is the longest we've been apart except for holidays …'

'Yes, I suppose it is,' Megan agreed.

'And didn't you miss me?' Peter coaxed.

Megan's heart sank. How could she tell him she honestly hadn't given him more than a fleeting thought – and even that had been mainly in anger?

'Well, I've been really busy …' she hedged, then took the bull by the horns. 'And anyway, I think we had been seeing too much of each other.'

'Well, I don't think we were.' He trapped her hand with his own, and this time she didn't try to withdraw it. 'I think we just saw each other the wrong way. Look, you've been brave enough to change your appearance – and I do like it, Meg, honestly – and I think if we changed a few other things, our relationship would be so much better.'

'What sort of things?' She looked into his earnest face,

trying hard not to think about Luke Dolan's blue eyes. 'Not see each other so much, do you mean?'

'No, I don't – oh!' He sighed as the waitresses arrived with the pudding course. 'I'll tell you later,' he muttered.

The speeches seemed interminable as Mitch and Jacey, their arms entwined, sat politely through them.

'Oh, thank goodness we don't have this sort of palaver with stock cars!' Jacey sighed. 'It's all so pompous! By the way, have you told your mum and dad about going to the race meeting at Warwick yet?'

'Not yet.' He twisted a strand of her hair round his fingers. 'They're used to me racing locally – but I haven't broken the news about the away fixture yet. What about yours?'

She lifted his hand and kissed it. 'Oh, mine were fine – they always are. They just said not to kill myself, because they couldn't afford the funeral – like they always do. I said it would mean a weekend away, and they just laughed and asked if you were going.'

'And?'

'I said yes and Mum said I'd probably be away for at least a week, then.'

Mitchell shook his head. Not for the first time, he wished his own parents would treat him with the same free and easy attitude.

The speeches over, the band returned to the podium, and couples began to drift on to the floor.

'I can't dance to this!' Jacey giggled. 'I thought they'd have a disco.'

'Not a hope.' Mitchell held out his hand. 'Come on, Miss Brennan. I'll teach you.'

'You can't waltz!' Jacey grinned, melting into his arms. 'Can you?'

'Of course I can waltz. Gran Phillips taught us all how to

waltz, how to play poker, and how to mix cocktails at an early age. She said that would cover us for every eventuality.'

Megan and Peter had also taken the floor. Peter danced stiffly, with very little sense of rhythm, but Megan was used to it.

She closed her eyes, allowing herself to dream of being in Luke's arms ...

'Hi – Megan?' Her brother's voice made her eyes snap open. 'You look incredible.'

'Thanks.' Megan smiled warmly at him. 'Hello, Jacey.'

Jacey grinned. 'That's a first. A member of the Phillips family speaking civilly to me!'

Megan pulled a face. 'We're not that bad, are we?'

'Pretty daunting.' Jacey giggled as they waltzed apart again, and she looked up at Mitchell. 'At least – most of you are ...'

She's – very – er –' Peter frowned as Mitchell and Jacey disappeared in the throng.

'Very what?' Megan snapped, feeling jealous of the way Mitchell and Jacey looked at each other. 'Happy? In love?'

'Common, actually,' Peter said with a disapproving sniff. 'I know that's what your parents think.'

'No, they don't!' Megan protested. 'They just think she's wild and headstrong and wrong for Mitchell – but I don't. I think they're made for each other.'

'Like we are?' Peter whispered. 'Meg, what I was trying to say to you earlier was ...' He swallowed. 'Oh, look, Megan, will you marry me?'

Megan was sure her jaw had dropped. She wanted to laugh and cry at the same time.

'Well?' Peter had stopped dancing and was holding her close. 'What about it?'

'I – er – I don't know what to say.'

She didn't want to hurt him by refusing him point blank – and yet, wasn't that the kindest thing to do?

Peter was speaking again. 'I'm seeing Mr Bamford next week about promotion, like you suggested.' He was smiling, excited. 'Even if it means moving to one of the Oxford branches and not staying in Appleford. I've thought over everything you said, Megan. I'll get a good mortgage discount because of working at the bank, and we can buy one of those new starter homes on the Merlin estate, and then –'

'Hang on!' Megan felt panic rising in her chest. 'You can't have made all these plans without me!'

'I've done nothing else all week.' Peter pulled her even closer. 'I've been thinking how to make you happy. You were the one who said I was unambitious, after all.'

'Was I?' Megan couldn't remember exactly what she had said, but she was pretty sure it hadn't involved marriage and mortgages and one of those little boxes on the Merlin estate. 'I don't think I meant –'

'Come on, you two lovebirds!' His mates Neil, Nigel, and Toby, with their wives in tow, bore down on them. 'The music's stopped. Last one to the bar buys the round!'

Whooping like schoolboys, they bounded across the dance floor and Peter moved to follow them.

'We'd better go, otherwise I'll have to pay for all their drinks – and I can't really afford that now, can I?' he said with a conspiratorial smile.

'Peter ...' Megan swallowed. 'I don't think –'

'Goodness!' Peter laughed. 'You can't be that surprised! You must have known I'd ask you to marry me one day, Meg. After all, we've always been together. There's never been anyone else.'

No, Megan thought, there hadn't been. And there still wasn't – because she couldn't count Luke's kiss as anything other than a moment of madness.

But she knew that, feeling as she did, there was no way she could accept Peter's proposal.

'Look,' he was going on, 'I'll give you a little bit of time to mull it over. Decide whether you want a long engagement or just arrange the wedding. Talk to your parents. You could even go down to the Merlin estate and have a look at the show houses! But I'll want your answer by next Saturday. All right?'

'All right,' Megan said weakly. 'Look, you'd better get to the bar. Neil's shoved his way through to the front and you know what he's like – they'll all be ordering doubles at your expense!'

Peter grinned. 'They would, too! But where are you going?'

'The cloakroom. If you've managed to get served before I get back, I'd like an orange juice.'

Megan watched him shouldering his way through the throng, and hated herself. Why hadn't she told him the truth? Now it was going to be harder than ever.

One thing was certain – she would tell him before next weekend that there wasn't going to be any wedding. She couldn't keep him dangling.

Wearily she pushed open the door of the ladies' cloakroom and Jacey turned from the mirror, her mascara brush poised.

'Hi! It's quite good, isn't it? I thought it would be really stuffy but it's livened up nicely. Not that the rugby club is my scene, of course, but …' She stopped and gazed intently at Megan. 'What's up? You look rotten.'

'Thanks.' Megan sketched a small smile. 'I feel rotten.'

'You're probably working too hard.' Jacey returned to brushing her eyelashes. 'Mitchell says you drive taxis all the time.'

Thoughtfully Megan surveyed her new image in the harsh fluorescent light.

'That's true, I suppose. But I love it. I enjoy meeting people and talking to them. They tell me all sorts of things.'

Jacey had finished her eyes and was concentrating on her luxuriant hair but she glanced at Megan in the mirror.

'What, all of them?'

57

'Well, not so much the busy mothers I pick up from the supermarket,' Megan agreed. 'But the older people always like to tell you about their day – even if they're only going to the doctor. And the tourists who stay in Appleford and want to do Oxford's sights are interesting, too.'

'I'd enjoy that.' Jacey gave her a smile of real friendship. 'I'm dead nosy – and that way it wouldn't be prying, would it? It would be part of the job.'

Megan laughed in agreement. She couldn't understand why people didn't like Jacey Brennan, and could absolutely understand why Mitchell did.

Jacey snapped her handbag shut.

'You still look like you could do with a break, though,' she went on. 'You know what they say about all work and no play. Look, Mitch and I are racing at Warwick next weekend – why don't you come along? Bring Peter Thingy if you want to –'

'I couldn't,' Megan answered quickly. 'And anyway, Peter will be playing rugby.'

'Give yourself a little holiday, then,' Jacey said gaily. 'Come on your own. You could help me with my car – one of my brothers usually does it but he's working next weekend. We could go for female solidarity – an all-woman team!'

Megan was about to refuse, but Jacey's enthusiasm suddenly got to her, and she grinned.

'Why not? I'd love to. Mitch has all the details, has he?'

'Yes – but he hasn't told your parents yet.'

'OK.' Megan nodded. 'I'll be discreet.'

A crowd of rugby wives and girlfriends surged into the cloakroom at that point, and Jacey left to join Mitch.

Megan looked at the unfamiliar hair in the mirror, and wondered why both she and Mitch were being economical with the truth.

Peter had been served once she reached the bar and was

waving an orange juice.

He beamed at her. 'I haven't told a soul! We'll announce it next weekend. I thought we could invite both lots of parents down to the Blue Boar. The whole team will be there and we can tell everyone at the same time.'

Megan felt her heart contract with panic.

'Peter – next weekend isn't such a good idea. Actually, I've just been talking to Jacey and –'

'I wish you wouldn't,' he said, sliding a proprietorial arm round her shoulders. 'I must say I agree with your mum about that girl. And she's hardly a suitable companion for a prospective bank manager's wife – is she?'

Annoyed, Megan pulled away from him.

'Don't be such a snob! She's a friendly, honest girl. OK, she might be a bit unconventional in her behaviour and her appearance, but once you get to know her –'

'Which I don't intend to do!' Peter laughed, not at all annoyed. 'So, as I was saying, about next weekend –'

'I'm not going to be –' Megan started, but her voice was swamped by a drum roll from the band.

'Oh – great!' Peter's cronies all swarmed forward. 'It's the silly session! Come on, Meg – don't be a party pooper!'

Megan could have stamped in frustration as she found herself dragged between Peter and Toby into something that could only be described as a rugby scrum to music.

I'll have to tell him later, she thought as she was whirled giddily from person to person. On the way home I'll tell him, when we're on our own.

'That's it, Megan!' Nigel panted as they executed a sort of *pas de deux* in the middle of the circle. 'Join in!'

She caught a glimpse of Mitch and Jacey, still sitting at their table, looking at the mayhem with amusement, and suddenly she wanted to be as far away from the rugby club as possible.

'What's up?' Peter yelled as they met in a whirl. 'Don't

you feel well?'

'No – I've got a headache.' Megan winced as the scrum danced around her. 'Would you mind if we went?'

'Went?' He was dancing with Neil's wife, Jenny. 'Go home, you mean? Oh, Meg, no! It's just getting warmed up!'

'Please, Peter. We need to talk –'

'Talk later!' Nigel shouted in her ear. 'Enjoy yourself!'

'Peter!' Megan felt tears stinging her eyes. 'Please!'

Laughing, Peter shook his head.

His team-mates were watching the exchange with interest, and Megan shrugged.

'OK. I'm sure someone will drive you back, Peter, but I'm going …'

She almost expected him to follow her, but when she reached the doorway and looked over her shoulder, he was still laughing uproariously with his mates.

Megan shook her head. She wasn't surprised. It was the way it had always been.

Grabbing her coat, she hurried out into the cold night.

The drive back to Lavender Lane took very little time. It was a clear night with frost already dusting the verges, and the roads were deserted.

The bungalow was practically in darkness and Megan sighed. She would have loved to curl up by her parents' fire to tell them about Peter's proposal – and her doubts. But it looked as though they were having an early night.

There was a light in Matt and Sally's living room. They were probably watching the late film, maybe with Kim cuddled between them on the sofa.

The thought of her niece, all drowsy and warm, made Megan smile. She'd just pop in for five minutes. Matt would understand.

She picked her way across the frosted path to Matt's front door but as she raised her hand to knock, she stopped in her tracks. She could hear Matt's raised voice – but not his words – and then Sally's rather shrill and obviously tearful reply.

Megan pulled a face. Not a good time for a visit! But as she turned she couldn't help hearing what her sister-in-law was shouting.

'I don't care why you did it, Matt! You can talk all night and I still won't understand. What I do understand is that your parents will kill you when they find out!'

Chapter Four
'Matt, How Could You?'

It was Tuesday afternoon. The wind howled round the bungalow beneath a low, yellow sky, and Lavender Cabs were run off their feet. Everyone wanted taxis. No one could face that biting wind, not even to wait for a bus.

Amy paced up and down her parents' living room, clenching and unclenching her hands. Not only was she dreading this confrontation with her sister and brother-in-law, but she was worried about Megan and Matt.

Megan had told her parents about Peter's proposal – and they had said, Amy thought, all the right things in the circumstances. But then Megan had burst into tears, mumbled that she didn't know what she wanted any more, and fled from the room, leaving her parents staring after her helplessly.

And Matt … Amy shook her head.

Matt and Sally had taken Kim and gone to London. For a break, Matt had said, white-faced, but while Sally had said nothing, her red-rimmed eyes spoke volumes.

Bob had protested that Lavender Cabs was really busy, it wasn't the best time for anyone to take a break, but Matt had become so agitated that Amy had stepped in as mediator.

And now there was this.

'If they don't turn up soon, Mum, I'll have to go. Bob's out driving with Matt being away, and Megan's manning the radio. We're really pushed.'

Amy's father grinned from the depths of his armchair

beside the fire.

'Don't go complaining about too much work, lass. And Judith and Paul will be here soon – don't fret. She was adamant on the phone. She said it had to be this afternoon. They've got something to tell us.'

Amy sighed. 'Please let it be that Paul has got a fabulous job offer in the Outer Hebrides and that all four of them will be packing their bags!'

Stella Foster laughed. 'Amy! This is your sister we're talking about.'

'I know.' Amy sighed. 'Sorry, Mum. I just don't think I can cope with another whinge about me and Bob having done them out of their inheritance.'

'That makes three of us.' Jim tapped out his pipe on the mantelpiece. 'I'm glad they've decided that they want to bring it all out into the open. Listen – is that their car?'

Stella bustled to the window. 'Yes, and they've got Debbie and Dean with them – looking as sulky as ever.'

'I don't know why they don't let those poor kids get on with their lives! Let Debbie go to art school and Dean study music, like they want to,' Amy said. 'They must be thoroughly cheesed off with being dragged into this.'

'They're not bad kids, considering, but I'm glad Paul wasn't my father,' Jim growled.

Amy hugged him. 'So am I. I've the best dad in the world – and the best mum, of course.'

Jim beamed, and Stella was smiling as she hurried into the hall.

Paul bustled in, the collar on his sheepskin jacket turned up, and rubbed his hands. 'Nice and warm in here, Dad. Hello, Amy.'

'Hello.' Amy forced a smile. 'I think it'll snow before the day's out.' Judith pressed her cheek against her sister's.

'I know you're busy, Amy, so we won't keep you.'

Amy noted that the whole family looked happier than she

had seen them look for a long time.

'The kettle's on,' Stella announced. 'Sit yourselves down.'

Dean and Debbie, looking out of place and wary, perched on the edge of the sofa and everyone else found a chair.

'We won't waste anyone's time,' Paul said in his parade-ground voice. It had probably commanded great respect during his army career but now only served to set Amy's teeth on edge.

'We'll put our cards on the table.'

'Shares, actually,' Judith giggled and everyone looked at her.

'Yes, well.' Paul took back the initiative. 'As I understand it, shares in Lavender – both the taxi business and the garage – were divided with Bob and Amy holding forty-nine and Jim and Stella fifty-one. On Jim's retirement, he held one share only and divided the others up between the Phillips children –'

'Yes,' Amy said. 'We've been through all this a hundred times …' She didn't like the way Judith was smiling.

'– with Megan and Matt each receiving twenty shares and Mitchell having the remaining ten?' Paul went on as though without interruption.

Jim nodded, and Stella leaned forward.

'But Mitchell didn't want to be a shareholder, so Jim and I hold eleven in all. Bob and Amy are majority shareholders, with Megan and Matt holding the balance. There isn't any room for negotiation, Paul. We divided the business up as we saw fit.'

'Yes, of course.' Paul grinned. 'That's all water under the bridge. We've solved the problem our way.'

'Thank goodness for that!' Jim lit his pipe, resting his head back in his chair. 'Go and make that tea, Stella, and maybe we can all start behaving like a proper family again.'

Amy, watching her brother-in-law closely, had a sense of foreboding.

'How exactly have you solved the problem, Paul?'

'It was very simple.' Judith gave the tinkling laugh that had irritated Amy from childhood. 'Maybe if you spent more time with your children, Amy, as we do with ours ...' She smiled at Dean and Debbie, who didn't meet her eyes.

'Get to the point, Judith.' Stella glared at both her daughters. 'You're grown women with families – not little girls squabbling over hair ribbons!'

'We now own twenty shares in Lavender!' Judith's words rang out triumphantly. 'And we're here to tell you how we intend to use them.'

Silence invaded the room. Only the fire was brave enough to make a sound until Jim's pipe fell into the hearth with a clatter, breaking the spell.

'Sally has been wanting to start her own business for some considerable time,' Judith explained. 'But because of this notion that the Phillips family can only be involved in Lavender, she's been unable to do so. We – um – helped her out of that situation ...'

'No!' Amy jumped to her feet. 'Not Matt? You haven't ...?'

'He didn't take much persuasion,' Judith said quietly. 'He was desperate to keep Sally happy, to keep his marriage together. We gave him a fair price. Certainly enough for them to start this aromatherapy thing that Sally's so keen on ...'

Stella and Jim sat looking stunned. Amy could feel the tears burning her eyes. So that was why Matt and Sally had decided on their impromptu holiday! She felt sick. Why on earth hadn't Matt told her? No, that was obvious. He'd known only too well how she and Bob would react.

'But we would have to have been, told, surely?' Amy protested. 'The other shareholders would have to agree, wouldn't they?'

'Not unless it was going to alter the balance of power,' Stella explained, her eyes cold as she surveyed her son-in-law. 'I assume you took legal advice?'

'Naturally. It was all done through our solicitor. Matt will carry on driving for Lavender, of course,' Paul said. 'He'll also be employed on the garage side. He'll simply take a salary – as Mitchell does. It seems as though your children, Amy, aren't quite as keen on Lavender Cabs as you are,' he added in a sneering tone.

'We'd like Debbie and Dean to become involved in the business,' Judith went on. 'I'll help out as and when, and we'd like to suggest that Paul becomes marketing manager ...'

'What?' Jim roared, jerked out of his stunned silence. 'Lavender doesn't need a marketing manager!'

'Oh, but it might,' Paul said quietly, 'if we're going to interest the big boys. This is our opportunity to drag Lavender where it belongs – into the twenty-first century. Into the world of multi-retailing, fast food, promotions –'

'Never! Not as long as I've got breath in my body!' Amy looked wildly at her parents. 'Mum – Dad – tell him!'

Stella's eyes were filled with tears, and Jim's face was grey. He took a deep breath and stared icily at Judith and Paul.

'Lavender stays as it is – as it's always been. You might be my family, but I will not let you destroy what I've built.' He stopped, swallowing his anger, and looked at Amy. 'Tell Matt I want to see him the minute he gets back.'

'And you're telling me you knew nothing at all about this?' Bob faced his mother over the kitchen table. 'You didn't have a clue what Matt and Sally were up to?'

It was Saturday morning, nearly a week after Matt and Sally had left for London, and Cicely had been as stunned as the rest of the family.

She sighed. 'I knew Sally was serious about the aromatherapy business – but I knew nothing about Matt selling his shares. For goodness' sake, he didn't need to!'

'He obviously thought he did,' Bob said wearily. 'And as

he did it legally, we're stuck with Paul and Judith – not to mention Dean and Debbie – whether we like it or not.'

Cicely looked at him, at the dark circles under his eyes and the lines etched on either side of his mouth. She knew that Amy looked even worse.

It was their son's deception that had hurt them, even more than the fact that Paul and Judith now had a say in the business.

She cursed herself for not telling Matt earlier that she would be financing Sally's Floral Oils.

'But can Lavender support four extra people?'

'Hardly!' Bob gave a short laugh. 'But at the moment Paul is being very magnanimous, investing his army gratuity in the business. Just until we fall in with his money-making schemes, of course ...'

Cicely squeezed his arm. 'I honestly don't know where Matt and Sally are. I do know Sally has a potential supplier in London, someone she met on her course, but I don't know any names. But there is something I should say ...'

'What?' Bob raised his head. 'If there's anything that might help –'

'Sorry – this won't. But you ought to know that Matt didn't need to sell his shares to help Sally. I'd already bought the lease on that empty shop in the High Street. I was going to back Sally, go into partnership with her ...' He stared at her blankly. 'So why did Matt sell out? He must have known –'

'He didn't.' Cicely shook her head. 'Sally and I wanted to keep it a secret. We wanted it all to be cut and dried before anyone else in the family found out ...'

'What?' Bob roared, leaping to his feet and glaring at her. 'You actually encouraged Sally? Oh, Mother, you've gone too far this time! What on earth did you think you were doing?'

'Helping Sally!' Cicely glared back with equal ferocity. 'Because Sally means a lot to me, and she feels that Lavender is the only thing that matters to any of you. She wanted to be her own woman – and I recognised that need. And please don't roar at me, Bob. Us falling out will help no one.'

'No.' Bob slumped back into his chair. 'Sorry.'

They were gazing silently at the softly falling snow when Amy came in.

'It looks like it's going to settle,' she commented. 'Which makes my next bit of news even more helpful ...' she finished.

'Don't.' Bob groaned. 'Not engine trouble? Not an accident?'

'Nothing that dire!' Amy gave a tired smile. 'It's just that the other members of our family are defecting, too.'

Cicely and Bob stared at her.

'Apparently there's a stock car meeting in Warwick this weekend. Mitch, of course, is going – and so is Megan.'

'Megan?' Cicely's eyebrows rose. 'Good heavens! She's certainly taken this change of image to heart, hasn't she?'

'She's going as Jacey Brennan's second,' Amy said darkly, 'which in normal circumstances would bring me out in a rash. But I get the feeling that it has a lot more to do with avoiding Peter King than a sudden desire to hurtle round a snow-covered track in a clapped-out car.'

'You're laughing!' Bob made it sound like an accusation, although his own eyes were twinkling. 'You don't want Megan to marry Peter at all, do you?'

'No,' Amy admitted, and sat down to help herself from the earthenware teapot. 'If only Mitchell would leave Jacey, and Matt would come back and tell us that it was all a mistake – and Paul and Judith could be captured by an alien spaceship – I'd be the happiest woman on Earth!'

They all laughed, the first time anyone had laughed since Tuesday.

Bob decided not to tell Amy about Cicely's involvement in Sally's business yet. Right now, he was delighted to see some of the tension melting from her face.

'Well,' he commented, 'if our children can do it – why don't we? You were saying that you wanted a break, love. Why don't we just up sticks and go?'

'That's very tempting,' Amy conceded, 'but you know it's impossible right now – though I'll hold you to it once everything's sorted out. But I've got an even better idea.'

Cicely smiled at them both and stood up.

'I'll go and say goodbye and good luck to the youngsters while you two cook up your nefarious plan.' She shrugged on her sheepskin jacket, then paused in the doorway to look seriously at them. 'It'll all work out, you know. Life has a habit of sorting out its own convolutions. Things look bleak at the moment – but this time next year you'll look back and laugh.'

Amy and Bob looked at her retreating figure and grinned at each other.

'There goes the eternal optimist!' Bob observed, and sat back in his chair. 'Still, interfering old busybody though she is, at least she makes us smile. Now, what's this cunning plan of yours that's going to help Lavender cope with the busiest weekend since Christmas?'

'I think it's about time our newest shareholders earned their keep.' Amy swirled the dregs of her tea round in the cup. 'We're going to be without all three of our children, so Paul can take over Matt's driving and help you out. Judith can cover for Megan, driving the supermarket and Oxford pick-ups. Dean can start getting his hands dirty in the garage – and Debbie can begin to learn the radio with me in the office. Let's see how delighted they are with their new-found status by the end of tomorrow night!'

Bob grinned. 'That's the sort of wicked scheme I'd have expected from Mother! But it's a brilliant idea! They'll be completely exhausted!'

'I do hope so.' Amy smiled slowly. 'It seems we're stuck with them for the time being, so let's show them what hard work Lavender really is!'

70

Standing at the window, Bob watched as Cicely carefully picked her way across the yard towards the garage, and hoped that she was right. He hoped that in a year's time all this would be sorted out.

He knew that when Matt returned trouble would start again in earnest, but in the meantime, he was looking forward to watching Paul and Judith having to work for their living.

He grinned as Cicely tugged the garage doors open with a strength that belied her age, and called into the depths, 'I've just come to say goodbye – and good luck!'

Mitch, securing his car on to its trailer, looked up with a grin.

'Thanks, Gran. It'll be strange not having you cheering me on this afternoon.'

'Well, I've never considered myself a fair-weather supporter.' Cicely rubbed her hands together. 'But I don't think even my thermals will stand up to these Siberian conditions! Are you coming straight back?'

Mitch shook his head and indicated the far side of the garage where Megan and Jacey were checking their pink and lilac car.

'We thought we'd make a weekend of it. We've booked into a guest house. It should be good fun.'

Megan came over and kissed Cicely's cheek.

'I'm really looking forward to this – for all sorts of reasons! How are things with Mum and Dad?'

Cicely smiled. 'Improving. Don't worry, Meg, I'll keep an eye on them. It's about time you had some fun. Just bring these two home in one piece!'

'Right. All set?' Jacey flicked her long blonde hair away from her face. 'We ought to get going as soon as possible with this weather.'

'I'm all ready.' Mitch enveloped her in a hug. 'If you take Meg with you, Luke can come with me.'

Megan's eyes widened. 'Luke?'

'Yes.' Luke grinned as he emerged from the office, pulling on his battered leather jacket. 'I've just phoned Warwick. The meeting's still on as long as the snow doesn't get any worse.'

Megan knew she was blushing. She looked at the smiling faces and swallowed.

'You mean – you're coming with us? For the whole weekend?'

Chapter Five
An Enchanted Evening

Megan stepped from Jacey's car, shivering in the icy wind. The stock car circuit looked surprisingly pretty with its light encrusting of snow.

'As long as we don't have any more, it should be an exciting meeting,' Jacey said casually, and Megan looked at her in admiration.

'Aren't you ever scared?'

'Petrified.' Jacey grinned cheerfully. 'That's half the fun. Come on, let's go and see how the boys are doing.'

Despite her misgivings about Luke's presence, Megan had thoroughly enjoyed the drive to Warwick. She had felt her spirits lift as soon as they had got on to the motorway. They were four friends off for an exciting weekend. She couldn't remember when she had last felt this zing of exhilaration.

This was what being young was all about, she thought, as she and Jacey slithered towards the pits. Not being towed in Peter King's wake, being bored rigid by rugby, and irritated by the infantile behaviour of his friends.

'There's a huge crowd!' Mitch looked up from last-minute checks on his car. 'And the track is clear. I've got a good feeling about this one.'

'A good feeling about coming second,' Jacey teased. 'Because this is one race that I'm going to win.'

'We'll see about that!' Mitchell laughed. 'Anyway, whoever loses will be buying the drinks tonight!'

'Looks as though you and I will be treated whatever

happens, Meg.' Luke grinned at her. 'Anyway, once you've got Jacey's car on the track, come back round here. Then you'll be on the spot if she needs any repairs or anything.'

Megan nodded, not meeting his eyes. This was ridiculous, she told herself. She'd known Luke for ages, and that kiss, devastating as it was to her, had meant nothing to him, she was sure it hadn't. Therefore she had decided to act towards him as she always had – friendly and detached – so why was she behaving like a gauche teenager the minute he smiled?

'Let's go!' Jacey grabbed her arm. 'The marshals are out on the track – it won't be long now.'

Within half an hour the icy air was torn apart by the roar of twenty engines. Watching Mitch's red car, decorated with fire-breathing dragons, nudge towards the start line alongside Jacey's pretty pastel and hearts, Megan pulled on her gloves and hurried to the pits.

She leaned on the snow-covered railings, her face whipped by the biting wind, and Luke grinned.

'Never fancied doing this yourself?'

'Absolutely not. I've got a great sense of self-preservation! What about you?'

'I'd love to, but at the moment the money doesn't stretch to it. Anyway, I'm quite happy playing second fiddle.'

Megan shot him a sharp glance, but his face was innocent.

Before she could say anything else, the flag had been raised and the roar of the engines made speech impossible.

The race was even more manic than usual because of the conditions. Cars were sliding and spinning everywhere as if on a dodgems track.

'I reckon Mitch could win!' Luke shouted in her ear. 'There's only one more circuit to go and he's in a good position!'

'So's Jacey!' Megan shouted back. 'They're neck and neck!'

The pits were littered with cars that had bitten the dust, and most of the drivers were leaning over the pit rails, howling encouragement.

Megan and Luke exchanged grins as Mitch and Jacey, locked together, rounded the last bend.

'It looks as though Mitch will be footing the bill tonight.' Megan laughed. 'Jacey's going to win.'

She did, by a whisker. The crowd were ecstatic – especially when they realised that the winner was a very pretty girl.

Jacey proudly collected her trophy, and everyone laughed as Mitch was the first to congratulate her.

'All I need now is a hot bath, a good meal, and a wild evening's entertainment,' Jacey told Megan as they followed Mitch's car away from the stock car circuit. 'We'll have to keep close to Mitch,' she went on. 'He's the only one who knows where the guest-house is. Thanks for your help this afternoon – you were brilliant.'

'I loved it.' Megan smiled back, knowing now this friendship was cemented for ever. 'Maybe we could make it a regular thing.'

'That'd be great. I can't believe I ever thought you were stuck-up and distant,' Jacey said with an apologetic smile as she drove carefully through the snow, keeping a safe distance behind Mitch but never letting him out of her sight. 'It just goes to show you should never judge on appearances, doesn't it?'

It did, Megan thought. She had been guilty of that very thing herself.

'Oh, this must be it.' Jacey leaned forward and peered through the snowflakes at the sprawling red house with lights glowing warmly from the windows. 'Looks cosy, doesn't it?'

Mitch and Luke were already standing on the steps, their hair sequinned with snowflakes.

'We've only booked bed and breakfast,' Mitch said, 'so we'll have to find somewhere to eat. And the sooner the better. I'm starving!'

They trooped into the hall where their landlady was

waiting, smiling expectantly.

'Your rooms are all ready for you and there's plenty of hot water if you'd like baths or showers. You can make tea or coffee in your rooms and breakfast will be at nine.' Mitch thanked her and took the keys, throwing one to Luke.

'Oh, ha-ha. Very funny,' Megan said.

'Come on, Mitch. Where's mine?'

'Luke's got it.' Mitch's face was innocent. 'I booked two double rooms.'

Megan felt herself blushing scarlet and was thinking desperately about sleeping in the car or catching the train home when Luke laughed.

'That's enough, Mitch. Can't you see Meg's about to turn tail and flee?' He smiled gently at Megan. 'There are two rooms – one for you and Jacey, the other for me and your rotten brother!'

As Megan smiled gratefully at Luke, Mitch punched him playfully on the shoulder.

'She obviously isn't going to be succumbing to your charms! Come on – I'll race you for the bathroom!'

'You'll lose that one, too!' Jacey shouted, scampering along the corridor.

An hour later, showered, changed, and starving, they were all in the hall again.

'Jacey and I fancy a pizza and a noisy pub,' Mitch said. 'Is that all right with you two?

Megan's heart sank. 'Not for me.' Luke shook his head. 'I fancy something more substantial – and I'm sure Megan does, too. After all, we're not running on adrenaline like you two. How about if we find somewhere more sedate to eat and meet up with you later? Is that all right, Megan?'

'Lovely,' she agreed, thinking how nice it was to be asked for a change. Peter always just assumed. 'You two can go and discuss carburettors over your pizza while we –'

'– discuss the world situation, monetary policy, and the

financial viability of Lavender Lane under new management!' Mitch teased. 'How boring.'

Still laughing, he and Jacey clattered out of the guest house.

'Thank you.' Megan smiled at Luke. 'I sometimes feel flattened by their exuberance. But I don't want you to go to any trouble for me. I mean …'

'Meg – shut up,' Luke said kindly.

'I've been trying to get you on your own all day, and I really do need something to eat. All right?'

She couldn't help but return his smile.

They went out into the street, and Megan sighed, entranced by its crystalline beauty. Snow was still falling softly, looking like swirling feathers in the amber glow of the street lamps, and all the buildings had been softened by a blanket of white.

Luke looked at her anxiously. 'Shall I go back for the car?'

'Oh no! I love the snow. I'd much prefer to walk.'

Luke grinned. 'It could be a long way! I haven't a clue where we're going.'

Megan didn't care. She couldn't think of anything nicer than walking through the snow in this lovely old town with Luke at her side.

Hands linked, steadying each other, they set off in the direction of the castle.

'Careful,' Luke warned her. 'It looks pretty treacherous …'

'I know I'm older than you, but I'm not quite in my dotage! I can manage – oops!' Suddenly her feet shot from under her.

Laughing, Luke caught her, and for a second she was held tightly against him, her face buried in the soft leather of his jacket.

She lifted her face and wordlessly they stared at each

other before he bent his head and kissed her, his lips sweet-chilled by the snow.

Megan wound her arms round his neck, knowing now what she had suspected before.

'Meg,' he whispered. 'Oh, Meg ...'

She moved her icy cheek against his and smiled as the snowflakes tumbled in a white cloud around them. He pulled her even closer.

'Megan Phillips – I love you.'

Cicely stepped from the train at Paddington and straightened her hat. Because of the snow, the journey had been much slower than she had anticipated.

She looked around at the early evening bustle and sighed. It was all so different from those elegant days of travelling to London by steam train when they'd had proper carriages, with net luggage racks, richly upholstered seats, and framed pictures of Welsh mountains and Scottish lochs on the walls. Now, she thought, tugging her overnight bag more firmly on to her arm, it was as impersonal as an airport.

She joined the queue for taxis. Even she blanched at the thought of travelling alone on the tube in the evening. She shook her head sadly. So many things had changed.

The queue moved quickly, and she settled back into her seat after giving the driver her destination.

Bob and Amy would have kittens if they knew she had come to London without telling them. She only hoped they wouldn't ring until tomorrow night, when she'd be safely back home.

The driver stopped outside the small West London hotel and opened the door.

'Mind how you go, love. The paths are a bit slushy. We'll be getting more snow before morning, I reckon.'

Cicely paid him, tipping handsomely as she always did, and he carried her bag into the hotel foyer.

'Mrs Phillips,' she told the receptionist. 'I've booked a room for tonight. I'm not too late for the dining room, am I? I did reserve a table and my guests may have arrived before me.'

The receptionist assured her with a smile that they would be delighted to see her in the dining room at any time up to ten thirty, that her guests had not yet arrived, and did she want assistance with her luggage?

Cicely looked down at her one bag.

'No, thank you, dear,' she said with a smile.

She was still smiling as she unlocked the door of her room. What a nice place! So friendly!

It hadn't taken a great deal of sleuthing to discover where Matt and Sally were staying, and it was so convenient – their hotel was close enough for them to join her for dinner.

In normal circumstances, she would have preferred not to have any of the family around on this very special evening, but Matt and Sally – and dear little Kim – were very important to her. It was her duty to try to pour oil on the troubled waters of Lavender Cabs and heal this rift in the Phillips family.

Of course, she thought as she removed her hat and coat, Sally and Matt had been very surprised to receive her telephone call telling them that she would be in town, and even more intrigued when she'd told them she wouldn't be alone. She chuckled to herself, wondering what their reaction would be. The youngsters weren't the only ones who could spring surprises!

She just had time to freshen up before she went down to the restaurant to meet her real reason for visiting London …

'I gather Gran arrived about an hour ago,' Matt told Sally as she settled Kimberley in her high-chair at the table. 'The head waiter says she'll be with us shortly. I wonder who she's got with her?'

Sally smiled as she sank into her own seat. 'She's so

79

amazing, it could be anyone! But I don't care as long as it's no one from home hell-bent on giving us a lecture on family responsibilities! She must have used a private detective to find us so quickly! I thought we'd been really discreet.'

Mark grinned. 'Never underestimate Gran Phillips. I learned that from childhood. She always knew absolutely everything that was going on, and we never knew how. All the same, I'm pleased she's here, whoever she's brought with her. It might soften the blow a bit once we get back home.'

Cicely, elegant in dark green wool dress, sat in the hotel's small bar and glanced at her watch. She knew Matt and Sally were waiting in the dining room, and she was waiting, too.

The door opened, Cicely looked up – and the years fell away.

'Sam!' She rose to her feet. 'Oh, Sam! You haven't changed a bit!'

'Neither have you!' The tall, sun-tanned man with silver hair clasped her hands tightly. 'I can't believe it! After all these years!'

Smiling, tears glistening, they hugged each other.

'Oh, goodness.' Cicely scrabbled for her handkerchief. 'I'm crying! I never cry …'

'You did once,' Sam said softly, in an accent that still had traces of West Country overlaid with American. 'So did I.'

'We were just children then.' Cicely dabbed at her eyes. 'And foolish.'

'And very much in love.' Sam steered her towards the bar. 'Have we got time for a drink before we go in to dinner? I really need some time to get used to being with you again before I start meeting your family.'

'Yes – yes.' Cicely smiled at the barman. 'My grandchildren are waiting for me in the dining room. I wonder – could you let them know that I won't be long?'

'Of course.' The barman nodded. 'And can I get you a drink?'

'Whisky for me,' Sam said and then looked gently at

Cicely. 'And unless my memory is fading, a gin and tonic for the lady.'

They took their drinks to a corner table.

'I didn't think this would ever happen.' Cicely's fingers trembled on her glass. 'All these years of writing to each other since we've been widowed ... how long is it? Ten years now?'

'Nearer twelve.' Sam drank his whisky with relish. 'And I thought I'd never see you again. I never thought I'd be flying back across the Atlantic, not at my age ... And your family? They know nothing about me?'

'Nothing,' Cicely agreed. 'After all, what could I tell them?'

'Not the truth, that's for sure!' Sam laughed. 'After all, it was pretty shocking ... At least I know all about them, thanks to your letters.' He paused, drained his glass and held out his hand. 'I never stopped loving you, Cicely, not even after I married Margie. Oh, we had a happy marriage – but you were always tucked away in a corner of my heart.'

'We have – a once-in-a-lifetime love.' Cicely swallowed. 'That's what you called it. A love that caused a scandal at the time ...'

Sam moved closer, still holding her hand.

'Yes. I was considered totally unacceptable by everyone – and you were engaged to be married to the vicar! Fairly meaty stuff by anyone's standards – let alone for a small Oxfordshire village in those days. Still, we did the decent thing ... and I've regretted it ever since.' He smiled down gently at her. 'But there must still be some people around Appleford who remember what happened between us?'

'Not many. I married David and became a very good, if slightly unconventional, vicar's wife. David was a wonderful man – he put it all down to youthful high spirits. We were probably a seven-day wonder.'

'And now look at us.' Sam laughed. 'We look like Darby and Joan! No one would ever suspect.'

'Especially not the family! My grandchildren take part in some pretty hair-raising activities, but I think what we got up to would make even them think twice.'

Sam nodded. 'You were the best wing-walker in the business! Nerves of steel. I fell in love with you on that first trip – you were never frightened.'

'I trusted you – and the plane, of course. Anyway, it was the most exhilarating moment of my life, that first flight.' She glanced at her watch. 'I really think we ought ...'

'Of course,' Sam agreed. 'We shouldn't keep your grandchildren waiting. How are you going to introduce me?'

'As an old friend from more than fifty years ago.' Cicely chuckled. 'They'll just have to let their imaginations fill in the gaps.'

'You haven't changed a bit, have you?' Sam slipped her hand into the crook of his arm. 'You're still mischievous. Still daring and unconventional. Still beautiful. Still utterly heartbreaking.'

'And still in love with you,' Cicely whispered as they left the bar. 'Some things never change.'

'Our lives are going to, though.' Sam squeezed her hand as they walked towards the restaurant. 'That is, as long as you haven't changed your mind.'

'Not this time.' Cicely returned the squeeze. 'But how they'll take it, I really don't know.'

Chapter Six
Disillusioned

'I've had enough of this!' Judith's strident tones echoed from the cab radio. 'I'm calling it a day!'

Amy flicked the switch on the intercom.

'Sorry, but you're not. There are two more fares waiting at the supermarket, and I've got three customers here in the office to go to Oxford. Sorry, Judith. It's going to be a long evening.'

'But it's snowing!' Judith's voice wailed. 'And everyone's wet and grumbling and –'

'That's what Lavender Cabs is all about,' Amy said firmly. 'You wanted to be part of it, and now you are. When you've finished at the supermarket and taken these people to Oxford, you can have a break.'

As she decisively flicked the radio switch off, Debbie, sitting beside her at the desk, looked at her with wide eyes.

'Goodness! No one ever speaks to Mum like that!'

'She'll have to get used to it,' Amy returned tersely. 'She and your dad wanted to be part of this business. Now's an ideal opportunity for them to learn that it's not all wine and roses.'

Debbie giggled, and Amy found herself warming to her. She and her brother weren't so bad. It wasn't their fault they had been spoiled rotten.

'Would you like to have a go on the radio now? All the taxis have their own numbers so you know who you're speaking to. The booking sheet is here with the diary, and it's all backed up on the screen. You can keep track of where they all are with this street map.'

'I can't!' Debbie shook her head. 'I'll make a mess of it!'

'Nonsense. All you have to do is speak as if you're on the phone. You'll soon get the hang of it …'

Amy watched as Debbie tentatively consulted the sheets.

'I'll go and make us some coffee. Oh, and at the same time, you'll have to answer the phone and take the book-ins.'

'What?' Debbie blinked in amazement. 'I'll need four pairs of hands and three mouths! I thought Mum and Dad said this was a doddle. Money for old rope. Dad said –'

'Did he indeed?' Amy's face was grim. 'No doubt he's thinking differently now.'

While she was making the coffee, Amy kept an eye on Debbie. Dressed all in black, her hair a profusion of rainbow spikes, and with a diamond stud in her nose, she certainly didn't look suited to office life.

However, despite her appearance, Amy found her niece gentle and unworldly, with a dreamy nature better suited to creativity than commerce.

'Thanks.' Debbie took the coffee gratefully. 'I've spoken to two of the drivers and it was all right – I think. Well, one of them was Uncle Bob, so he was very patient. And I've taken a phone call from Denchworth Drive. I've written it here …'

'That's fine. You're doing very well. Now, would you like to call up your father and find out his position?'

'No!' she retorted sharply. 'I mean, I'd rather you did it. They were furious about this, you know.'

Laughing, Amy punched out Paul's call sign. He didn't answer for ages.

'Were you out of the cab?' she asked briskly when he responded.

'No. Trying to get some sleep.'

'Sleep! Where on earth are you?'

'On the taxi rank outside the station, though I don't see any need for me to be here. There are plenty of other cabs …'

'Mostly from other companies!' Amy snapped. 'All waiting to meet the trains from London and Oxford! For goodness' sake, Paul! This is your livelihood now. Those passengers are Lavender's bread and butter – especially in this foul weather. Now, wake up and start to do some work!'

'You can't speak to me like that!' Paul spat. 'How dare you!'

'Because Bob and I own Lavender,' Amy said softly. 'And because although you own shares, you are not an equal partner. You've bought your way into this business, Paul, so you must pull your weight like the rest of us. I'll call you again in five minutes – and I'll expect to find you with a fare!'

When Amy turned from the console, Debbie was staring at her with saucer eyes.

'No one's ever spoken to Dad like that, Aunt Amy. I wish Dean could have heard you! You were wonderful!'

Amy grinned. She and Bob had run a tight ship all their lives, and she certainly wasn't going to carry any dead wood now – family or not.

The office door opened, and Judith, looking extremely angry, stomped in.

'I heard you talking to Paul,' she said icily, 'as did everyone else, and I'll thank you to have more respect! Is that how you treat your workforce, Amy? Because if it is –'

'No, it isn't,' Amy broke in. 'I never speak to any of the drivers like that, because I never have any need to. They're not only our employees but also our friends. That's how Lavender has always been run. We all work very hard, all of us, Judith. And that now includes you and Paul.'

Judith was quivering with anger.

'I'm going to speak to Mum and Dad tomorrow. This isn't what we expected, you know. We thought –'

'You thought you could buy your way in and change

Lavender into something completely different. But Appleford doesn't need a service station with a restaurant and a shop and a car showroom. Appleford needs a friendly, family-run garage and taxi firm – which is what they've got. And what they're always going to have. Now –' she smiled at her furious sister '– there's a Mr and Mrs Winterton and a Miss Higgins in the waiting area. They need to go to Oxford. When you've finished that, pop back in and have a cuppa. You look frozen.'

Amy and Debbie waited until Judith had stormed out of the office before looking at each other and exploding with laughter.

'Oh, Aunt Amy!' Debbie threw her arms round her neck. 'I do love you! Do you think you could adopt us? I haven't laughed so much for ages!'

Amy returned her niece's hug.

'Your brother's probably turned into a block of ice out in the garage. Go and give him a shout, Deb. Tell him the kettle's on.'

The radio crackled and Debbie stretched out a purple-fingernailed hand to answer it, but Amy shook her head.

'I'll get it. It's Bob's call sign. He's probably coming in for a cup of tea. You run and get Dean, love.'

As Debbie skipped happily out of the office, Amy grinned. She was so lucky. She and Bob had always been happy, always been content with each other and what they had. They were such good friends.

Tonight, she thought, as she reached for the microphone, they would get a take-away and a bottle of wine and sit by the fire watching the snow falling and talk and laugh and dream …

Maybe they would even watch that old film they'd recorded weeks ago. It had been popular during their courting days and they were looking forward to watching it again and reliving the memories. It would be a lovely evening …

The radio was still beeping insistently and Amy flicked

the switch.

'OK, Bob Phillips, I heard you the first time! Your radar's working well. We're just putting the kettle on – again. I'll dig out your mug – oh, and that goes for any of the rest of you who are in the vicinity and can spare a few minutes.'

'Amy!' The voice crackling into the office wasn't Bob's. 'It's Dennis. I'm in Bob's cab. Amy – there's been an accident. I was passing on the road by the railway cutting when I saw his car … he must have collapsed at the wheel. He's unconscious. I've called an ambulance. They're on their way but – Amy? Can you still hear me?'

'Yes.' Amy's mouth was dry. 'I can hear you. Dennis … is he …?'

Tears burned her eyes, and her hands were shaking. Everything was a long way away. Over the microphone she could hear the unearthly wail of the ambulance siren.

'Bob!' Her lips trembled the word.

'No! Please, no!'

The revolving blue light of the ambulance found an echo in Amy's brain. She felt sick with fear. Strong arms held her back from the taxi, but the light showed her all too clearly the shocking sight of Bob slumped over the steering wheel, with paramedics on either side of him.

Snowflakes fell gently all around the shadowy figures as they rushed backwards and forwards.

'He'll be all right,' Dennis, the driver who had found Bob, assured her over and over again. 'He's in good hands.'

'But what happened?' Amy asked numbly for the thousandth time.

Dennis shook his head. 'I've no idea. There wasn't another vehicle. Maybe he just skidded … He'll be able to tell us once they get him out.'

Would he? He was still unconscious. She had never felt so helpless, so alone.

'Mrs Phillips?' A young paramedic – he looked no older than Mitch – smiled kindly at her. 'We're going to take your husband to the Radcliffe. Would you like to come with us?'

Amy nodded, and Dennis touched her arm.

'Don't worry about your car. I'll get one of the other boys to pick it up. You go with him, Amy, and ring us as soon as there's news or if you want a lift home or – well, anything …'

Fresh tears welled in her eyes and wordlessly she squeezed his hand.

Bob was on a stretcher now, covered with a blanket on which the snowflakes were settling in incongruous beauty. There were wires and an oxygen mask, and everything looked efficient and frightening as they gently lifted him into the back of the ambulance.

She followed him in, staring as the paramedics checked dials and monitors.

'Sit here.' The young man indicated a seat beside Bob's stretcher. 'You can hold his hand on the journey – but we'll have to strap you in.' He gave a gentle smile. 'We shan't be observing the speed limit.'

The journey was something Amy would never forget. Sitting clutching Bob's frozen hand as the ambulance screamed through the darkness, she would always remember the jolting, the unearthly wail of the siren, the way that all the other traffic pulled over for them.

'We're going straight into A & E.'

The paramedics were lifting Bob almost before the ambulance had stopped. 'If you could go to reception and give them his details, Mrs Phillips? You'll be able to see him as soon as he's been examined.'

The bright lights hurt Amy's eyes as she pushed her way into the hospital.

Giving details to the receptionist seemed to take ages but finally she stumbled back to the waiting area. Everyone seemed to have someone with them … but the only person she wanted was unconscious in one of the cubicles.

'Mrs Phillips?' A dark-haired nurse was at her side. How young these wonderful people were, Amy thought blankly. 'Your husband has been examined. You can see him in a minute but the doctor would like a word.'

'Is he –?' The words died on Amy's lips. 'I mean ...'

'Mr Phillips is still unconscious.' She was already turning away. 'We'll be admitting him as soon as we have a bed. But the doctor will give you more details.'

Amy followed the neat, uniformed figure, vaguely aware of all the bustle around her, but completely untouched by it.

'Mrs Phillips?' The doctor, youthful and heavy-eyed, smiled at her briefly. 'I've examined your husband – er –'

'Bob.'

'Bob. He's showing all the signs of an angina attack, Mrs Phillips. I'm almost sure it wasn't a full-blown heart attack, but I'd like to keep him in for a few days for observation. We'll know more when he can talk to us, of course. Has he complained of chest pains, or been under undue stress recently?'

'No pains as far as I know,' Amy said quietly. 'But we're always under pressure. We run our own business and there have been family problems recently, too. He's not – not going to die, is he?' she whispered.

'Not if we can help it, but I think he'll have to take things very quietly for a while. No work, no upsets, no stress.' He looked as though he'd said it all a hundred times before. 'Is there someone we can contact for you? Someone who can wait with you?'

Amy shook her head. She didn't know where the children were, Cicely had disappeared, and her own parents would only get upset.

'No, thank you.' She swallowed. 'There's no one. I'll be fine. Can I see him?'

'Of course.' His tired eyes showed relief that she had taken it so well. 'He's through here. The nurses will be keeping an eye on him until we can get him up to the ward. I'll see you later, as soon as we can find a bed.'

Bob seemed asleep as she tiptoed to his bed. His face was pale, and his heartbeat was being monitored by yet another machine. The oxygen mask half-covering his face looked uncomfortable, and she reached over to ease it a little.

'I love you,' she whispered. 'Without you I'm nothing. Nothing else matters, Bob. Just you and me. Just you ...'

The tears flowed unchecked then, falling hotly down her cheeks. Leaning forward, she clutched his hand and rested her face against the hard pillow.

Time and reality lost all meaning. It could have been midnight or four in the morning.

The hospital was tropically warm and humming with life. The nurses came in, checked monitors, asked if she wanted tea, and went out.

'Amy?' It was Bob's voice, weak and hoarse. 'Amy – is there any chance of a cup of tea?'

Her cry brought the nurse scuttling through the curtains and Amy found herself firmly but kindly pushed to one side as the doctor arrived and the whole reassuring business of healing the sick moved smoothly into motion.

'If you'd like to wait outside, Mrs Phillips,' the doctor told her, 'we'll be moving your husband very shortly.'

Bob was moved quietly and efficiently to a dimly lit cubicle on the cardiac ward. Amy travelled up with him in the lift, holding his hand.

'Definitely angina.' The young doctor yawned and smiled apologetically. 'Sorry! It's been a long day! We'll keep him in for a few days, but with regular medication there is no reason why he shouldn't live a perfectly normal life. Of course,' he added, 'as I said, it will mean him keeping away from work for three or four months. He must have total rest. Someone else can take over the running of the business, I trust?'

'Hm? Oh – yes,' Amy muttered. Lavender Cabs was the last thing on her mind at the moment.

'Good. Remember, overwork and stress will only make matters worse. And next time it could be far more serious.'

Next time! Amy sank down beside Bob's bed in the soft darkness. There wasn't going to be a next time, she would make sure of that.

She would manage, wouldn't she?

Mitchell and Megan were hard workers, and the drivers were the best.

She would ask Matt to take over Bob's role. The fact that he had sold his shares was of no consequence now – she just wanted him to come home. She needed Matt. Lavender Cabs needed him.

Bob stirred in his sleep, and Amy smoothed his hair.

'It's going to be fine,' she promised him quietly. 'Just fine.'

Bob opened his eyes and smiled sleepily, and Amy bit her lip. She loved him more than life and his survival depended on her. Her life had been turned giddily on its head. Nothing would ever be the same again.

She felt alone and unbearably weary. The future suddenly looked very frightening.

'This is Sam.' Cicely beamed at Sally and Matt, with a special smile at Kimberley in her high chair. 'He's an old friend. Sam, my grandchildren, Matt and Sally, and my great-granddaughter, Kimberley ...'

Matt and Sally shook hands with him, and exchanged meaningful glances.

As soon as the courses had been ordered and drinks poured, Cicely sat back in her chair and raised her glass.

'Here's to new ventures. Here's to the future. Here's to Sally's Floral Oils – and to your return to Appleford, my dears.'

'You don't think we're doing the wrong thing, Gran?' Matt ventured.

Cicely shook her head. 'No, I don't. Mind you, I don't think you should have sold your shares to Paul and Judith – but I suppose I'm to blame for that. I should have told you earlier that I was financing Sally. But you do realise you have to go home and face the music?'

'Yes, Gran,' Matt said meekly, and Sam chuckled.

'A chip off the old block here, I think.' He looked at them both. 'Your grandmother never toed the party line either.'

'So we gather.' Sally grinned as the starters arrived. 'So, how long have you two known each other?'

'A very long time,' Cicely returned.

'And how come we've heard nothing about Sam before?' Matt smiled. 'Is he a dark secret from your past, Gran?'

Sam and Cicely looked at each other and said nothing, and Sally pounced on the silence.

'Oh, tell us! Please!'

Sam raised his eyebrows and shook his head.

'I've promised your gran I'll say nothing. Not that we've got anything to hide, mind you – but ...'

Cicely laid down her knife and fork.

'Sam was a friend and – er – colleague of your grandfather's.'

'Oh, so you're a clergyman?' Sally asked.

Sam roared with laughter. 'Indeed I am not! Your grandfather did have other interests.'

As the waitress cleared their plates,

Cicely took a deep breath.

'Tell them, Sam. But I'll interrupt if there are any embellishments – just the truth, please.'

'I don't think it needs any embroidering.' Sam grinned, covering Cicely's hand with his own – a gesture that wasn't lost on Sally.

He began to tell them the story, transporting them back through the years to a time between the wars when peace seemed never-ending and life for the young was completely carefree.

'Cicely was seventeen when we met. Beautiful, daring, funny, a dream come true – and already engaged to your grandfather. David and I had met at college and we had lots of things in common. He invited me to stay with him in Appleford one summer – and we found we had one more. Cicely.'

'Oh!' Sally's eyes widened. 'The eternal triangle!'

Sam shook his head. 'I didn't wear my heart on my sleeve, and we held honour in high esteem in those days. Cicely belonged to David and that was that.'

'So what happened? 'I remember listening to Gran and Granddad Foster talking about some old scandal,' Matt put in. 'I was fascinated because they kept lowering their voices when they thought I was listening. I knew it was about you, Gran, because they always called you Cissie when they didn't want us to know.'

'Typical!' Cicely smiled. 'Stella and Jim have always been so conventional. I really thought the whole thing had died a death. I didn't think anyone would remember …'

'So what did you do that caused Gran and Granddad Foster to still talk about it years later?' Matt pressed.

'I doubt if it was Sam and me by that late date,' Cicely said, smiling. 'It was probably one of my other misdemeanours. Well, what else can you expect from someone who –'

'Hey, who's telling this story?' Sam broke in, laughing. 'Well, apart from falling in love with your grandmother on the spot, I was also David's closest friend. It was an awful dilemma. I had accepted the hospitality of his family for the whole of the summer – so I either had to return home or find some other way of putting Cicely from my mind. Strangely, David provided that.

'We had both learned to fly at college – we were very daring – and I joined David's flying club. At least up in the clouds I had to concentrate on what I was doing rather than think about Cicely.

'Then I was approached by Lord Rudrum. He wasn't a real lord, of course,' Sam explained. 'He was a showman. He ran a flying circus. He was looking for pilots, and I jumped at the chance. I thought it would give me the opportunity to make a dignified exit from David's place and forget all about Cicely …'

'But you still couldn't forget her?' Sally asked hopefully.

'You underestimate your grandmother.' Sam stroked Cicely's hand. 'She didn't give me a chance. As soon as she heard about it, she contacted Lord Rudrum herself –' he paused '– and soon your grandmother, the seventeen-year-old fiancée of the future vicar of St Matthew's, became the best wing-walker in the business!'

Matt and Sally sat with their mouths open, and Cicely felt the tears welling. It was a lifetime ago – but it seemed like only yesterday.

'I loved it,' she said huskily. 'I also loved Sam. We were the most daring couple in England! Kindred spirits. I thought I'd kept it secret. Very few people in Appleford knew – at least, not until it was all over, and then it was only hearsay.'

'But – what about Granddad Phillips?' Matt looked at his grandmother with new eyes. 'What on earth did he think?'

'Actually, he was happy for me to wing-walk. He was a real dare-devil himself, and very proud of me. His parents, of course, were pretty sniffy. And he knew nothing about Sam and me being in love …'

'But you wouldn't leave him?' Sally's eyes were moist.

'Absolutely not.' Cicely shook her head. 'As Sam said, we had very high ideals in those days. I was engaged to a man of the cloth – it would have caused a huge scandal. And I did love David … quietly and comfortably. Not with the fireworks and high drama of when I fell in love with Sam, of course.' She sighed. 'But I became a very good vicar's wife, and we had a long and happy marriage.'

'And after the war I went to America and carried on flying,' Sam added. 'I married an American girl called Margie, though I never forgot my wing-walker ...'

'We've been writing to each other for years – since Sam's Margie died,' Cicely said quietly. 'But this is the first time we've met. So!' She sat back and looked at her grandson. 'Don't think that your generation is the only one that can have problems or be unconventional!'

'Oh, it's so romantic!' Sally whispered. 'I always knew you were different but I had no idea just how special! But weren't you ever scared?'

'Never.' This time Cicely squeezed Sam's hand. 'At least, not of the flying. I trusted Sam with my life, literally. But I was sometimes terrified of having fallen in love with him. The scandal ... the pain it might have caused ... Still, in the end, it all worked out happily.'

'And now you're back together.' Matt was beaming. 'And is this just a flying visit – if you'll pardon the pun – or is Sam back for good?'

'My home is still in America,' Sam said quietly. 'My heart is – well elsewhere. The future depends entirely on Cicely.'

'Yes, we've got plenty to talk about,' Cicely agreed. 'As you have, my dears. I hope this little break has enabled you to sort out exactly what you intend to do?'

'Yes, it has.' Matt leaned towards Sally. 'We've had time to realise that our marriage – and Kim – are more important than anything else. We've sorted out stockists for Floral Oils, and thanks to your financial backing, Gran, the money I raised from my shares doesn't need to go into the business.'

'So,' Sally joined in, 'when we go back to Appleford we're going to face Amy and Bob – apologise for the trouble we've caused by selling the shares – and tell them that we'll be leaving Lavender Lane altogether.'

'What?' Cicely frowned. 'Do you mean –?'

Matt grinned. 'We're going to use the money to buy a house. We're going to move out of the bungalow, leave Lavender Cabs, and start up completely on our own.'

'Bob and Amy will understand,' Sally said firmly. 'I'm sure they will.'

'To be honest, it doesn't matter if they object or not,' Matt said grimly. 'Nothing – absolutely nothing – will make me change my mind.'

Chapter Seven
Doctor's Orders!

Six days later, Bob was released from hospital. Amy, driving carefully on the frozen roads, brought him quietly back to Lavender Lane.

'Where's the welcoming committee?' He grinned across at her as they pulled up outside the bungalow. 'I expected banners, a band, and a troupe of dancing girls at least.'

'Peace and quiet,' Amy said firmly. 'That's what the doctor said, and that, Bob Phillips, is just what you're going to get.'

Taking his arm, she helped him inside. Though she was delighted to have him home, her heart was still heavy.

Matt, Megan, and Mitch had been wonderful. They had promised to do whatever they could, had visited the hospital full of cheering stories and run Lavender Cabs with a zeal that couldn't be faulted. But Amy hadn't been fooled.

Ever since Megan had returned from Warwick, she'd had a bright-eyed look and had refused all phone calls from Peter.

Matt and Sally, full of contrition over the sale of their shares, seemed to be acting a part in a play.

And Cicely, who never behaved as anyone expected, while naturally extremely concerned about her son's illness, seemed almost distracted.

Mitch was the only one behaving normally. He had thrown himself into showing Dean and Debbie the ways of the garage and the taxi business, and had also dealt very firmly with Paul and Judith, organising their driving shifts and keeping them away from Amy at all times. She had been very glad of his support.

'It's great to be home.' Bob stretched his legs out in front of the roaring fire. 'But I don't want to be a nuisance.'

'You won't be.' Amy perched on the arm of his chair. 'You can spend your recuperation doing something we've both neglected for some time!'

'Don't tell me.' Bob groaned. 'You want me to update the photo albums for the last twenty years. Or worse – sit here and polish all those little brass ornaments the kids used to buy us.'

'Nothing so mundane!' Amy laughed, hugging him. 'Although, come to think of it, that's not a bad idea. No, what you can do while you're languishing in luxury is become a proper father.'

'But I've always considered myself a perfect father!' he protested.

'We've been very lenient and easy-going parents.' Amy smoothed his hair away from his forehead. 'After all, that's our nature. And I think we've done a great job. The kids are our friends, and they really haven't given us any trouble. But that business with Matt and the shares brought it home to me that we haven't spent much time with them since they've grown up. We never really have time to stop and talk and listen, do we? The business has always had to come first. But now you're going to have oodles of time …'

'Don't I know it!' Bob sighed. 'I'll be screaming with boredom after the first week.'

'Not a chance!' Amy smiled. 'The kids know they've got a captive audience. You'll probably have to keep an appointment book!

'Seriously, Bob, Lavender will run as it's always done. I just can't help thinking that if we'd been available for Matt to talk to, we might have been able to prevent him selling out to Paul and Judith. We didn't know how desperate Sally was to start her own business, did we? And we didn't know much about Jacey Brennan until she was an established part of Mitch's life – and we certainly didn't know how upset Megan was about Peter King.'

'Bob Phillips – Agony Aunt!' Bob laughed, some colour returning to his pale cheeks. 'OK, then. But there's one thing I must have first …'

'You've taken your tablets?' Amy queried in concern. 'What else is there?'

'A cup of tea.' Bob smiled happily. 'A proper cup of tea made by my darling wife in my own kitchen. It'll be nectar after all those cups of unidentifiable liquid the hospital dished up!'

'Slave driver!' Amy kissed him. 'Don't get too used to this, Bob. You'll be making your own before long.'

For the first time since the accident, Amy was humming as she bustled into the kitchen.

'Dad's home.' Mitchell looked out of the garage windows. 'Mum's car's outside. Shall we go and see him?'

'Give them a few minutes together.' Megan, perched on the work bench beside the roaring heater, suggested. 'They'll probably both be a bit weepy.'

'And we've got things to discuss before we all barge in and swamp him,' Matt said. 'After all, this is a bit of a turning point for us all.'

'It certainly makes a change for us all to be together without hangers on, other halves, or outsiders,' Megan agreed. 'So where do we go from here?'

'Dad's going to need all the help he can get.' Mitch's face, for once, had lost its grin. 'So's Mum. The business is going to have to run smoothly so that he has no worries, and so that Mum can devote more time to looking after him. There'll have to be sacrifices.'

'Sacrifices?' Matt looked at him. 'What would you know about sacrifices, Mitch?'

'Well, I'll have to forget the stock car racing for a while. There won't be time to spend on that. Although –' he glanced

99

out of the window '– if the weather stays like this the meetings will be cancelled anyway. Either way, Luke and I will be able to spend more time in the garage.'

'And I'll have to abandon the rugby teas,' Megan said cheerfully. 'That'll be awful, won't it?' she added, not meaning it at all. 'I can take over Mum's shift on the radio and do some more driving.'

Mitchell grinned. 'Somehow that doesn't seem like much of a hardship. Less time with the awful Peter and more time with Luke!'

'Luke?' Matt noticed Megan blushing. 'Don't be ridiculous! He's far too young for her.'

Mitch laughed. 'You weren't at Warwick. They somehow got themselves separated from Jacey and me. Found some romantic candlelit bistro, so the story goes ... We didn't see them again until it was time to go home.'

'Mitchell!' Megan's face was scarlet. 'That's not true!'

'No – well.' Mitchell was unabashed. 'Luke did eventually creep into his bed in the early hours of the morning with a soppy smile on his face.'

'Luke?' Matt shook his head. 'For heaven's sake, Megan – at least Peter King has prospects! What sort of future could you have with someone like Luke? Don't even think about it. It would break Dad's heart if he had to worry about you –'

'Shut up!' Megan flared. 'You don't know what you're talking about. At least I'm still committed one hundred per cent, to Lavender Cabs. Which – as I don't need to remind you – is more than you and Sally ...'

Matt squared his shoulders. 'Don't bring us into it. We'd made our arrangements before Dad was ill. It's too late to change them now.'

'Of course it isn't.' Mitchell frowned. 'You don't have a choice, Matt. You know what Mum said. Dad isn't to have any worries.'

'And in the meantime I'm supposed to sit back and watch

all our plans go down the drain, am I?' His face was dark with anger. 'You two may be quite happy to let Lavender rule your lives, but I'm not. I've got a wife and a child. My first responsibility is to them.'

Mitchell shook his head in disbelief. 'You can't! Surely you can put this aromatherapy thing on ice for a while?'

'Not a chance. We spent all that time in London sorting out suppliers, and we've committed ourselves financially. The shop is almost ready, the stock arrives next week – and …' He trailed off.

'And what?' Mitch leaned towards him. 'And what, Matt?'

'Nothing.' Now was not the right time to tell Mitchell and Megan about the house on the new Larkspur estate that he and Sally had put down a deposit on. He'd have to tell his parents first – but not yet.

'Well,' Megan, ever the peace-maker between her brothers, spoke quietly. 'We all know what we have to do. Sally can surely run the shop with Gran Phillips without taking Matt away from Lavender. We'll manage just fine – as long as Dad isn't upset by anything, and Mum has more time to spend with him.'

'Paul and Judith can help out as well,' Matt said sullenly. 'I don't see what all the fuss is about.'

'What?' Mitch's voice echoed round the garage. 'You're priceless, Matt! If it hadn't been for you, we wouldn't have been saddled with Paul and Judith in the first place! They're a liability – not an asset.'

'Talk of the devil.' Megan looked out over the snow-encrusted garage forecourt. 'Or should that be devils? There they are now. But they're the last people Mum and Dad will want to see on his first day home! Quick, Mitch – go and stop them!'

Mitchell rushed to the door, his anger at Matt's selfishness simmering, so that he was just dying to tell his aunt and uncle exactly what he thought of him.

'Too late!' He slithered to a halt on the frozen ground. 'Mum's already answered the door!'

Megan peered over his shoulder, her face a picture of despair, watching as her aunt and uncle disappeared into the bungalow.

'I was going to ring you later with tomorrow's duties,' Amy said as her sister entered the hall. 'I don't think Bob's up to visitors yet. He's just having a snooze by the fire.'

Paul laughed with false heartiness. 'Oh, we haven't come to visit the sick. We didn't think Bob would want to be disturbed. But neither have we come to see what horrendous hours you want us to work tomorrow, Amy.'

'No.' Judith smiled. 'We've come to tell you how we intend to help you out of this dilemma.'

'What dilemma?' Amy's heart plummeted. 'We don't have a dilemma. If we all pull together to cover Bob's duties for a few months, we'll be fine.'

Paul pulled a face. 'If you mean getting the kids to help out more and having us driving round the clock, I can't possibly agree with you. That's a recipe for disaster.

'Let's face it, Amy. Bob's going to be out of action for some considerable time. You can't neglect him – and you simply won't have time to look after him and run the business. Nor do the children – yours or ours – have the sort of commitment you believe them to. I've heard whispers about Matt, you know – and Mitchell has already proved his unreliability. No –' Paul's smile showed very white teeth beneath his moustache. '– there's only one thing for it – and we've already discussed this with Mum and Dad Foster, who agree it's for the best.'

'It's all worked out well.' Judith's voice was a triumphant purr. 'Paul and I are going to take over the running of Lavender Cabs.'

Bob sighed, hearing the voices echoing from the hall. What on earth did Paul and Judith want, today of all days? He closed his eyes, hoping that Amy would be able to get rid of them. He didn't want to admit to anyone – not even Amy – just how weak he was feeling, and how much his illness had frightened him.

'... and I'm very sorry, too.' Amy's voice was firm. 'But now is not a good time. Bob has only just come home and a discussion on the future of the business is the last thing he needs. Anyway, the children are coping well, and I'll be back in the office tomorrow.'

Bob groaned and eased himself to his feet. Steadying himself against the furniture, he made slow progress towards the door and pulled it open.

Three heads turned and Amy frowned.

'Bob, I'm sorry. Go back and sit by the fire. Judith and Paul aren't staying.'

'Maybe they ought to.' Bob nodded at the visitors. 'Maybe we could get a few things sorted out and save any speculation.'

'That's just what we thought.' Paul was already shrugging himself out of his sheepskin jacket. 'Amy seems determined to protect you like a mother hen, but I think if we lay our cards on the table now, your recuperation will be that much quicker.'

Amy muttered under her breath, and Bob grinned.

'We were just going to have a cuppa. I'm sure Amy can stretch to two more.'

'Bob.' Amy's voice was low. 'This is exactly what the doctors told you to avoid.'

Judith walked quickly past her towards the kitchen.

'We've no intention of upsetting either of you! Let's leave the men alone for a moment, Amy. We'll talk out here while we make tea.'

Bob grinned again at the mutinous expression on Amy's face, and ushered Paul into the snug warmth of the living room. As he closed the door he heard Amy's voice: 'Why do I get the feeling that this has been carefully rehearsed, Judith?

Get on with it. But don't expect me to agree to anything.'

Bob sank back into his chair and motioned to Paul to take a seat.

'I'm glad to see you're looking so well,' Paul said heartily. 'You gave us all a nasty shock.'

Bob waited. He didn't have to wait long.

'I'll come straight to the point,' Paul said, shifting in his chair. 'You're going to be sidelined until the spring, Bob, and Amy would be better employed spending time with you. Neither of you needs the worry of Lavender at the moment. That's where we come in.'

Bob raised his eyebrows. 'I understood everything was running smoothly.'

'Yes, of course it is,' Paul agreed. 'But as there's no sign of a let-up in this appalling weather, and everyone wants taxis, all the drivers are stretched to the limit. The garage could run twenty-four hours a day with all the breakdowns and accident repairs we're being asked to do.

'More often than not that reception area is bulging with people – people who could do with a drink and a snack while they wait. People who would buy something to read. People who might even like to hire a car to tide them over ...' He leaned forward. 'Business opportunities by the score, Bob, which are simply going to waste.'

Bob leaned his head back in his chair. The wind was rattling the windows and the ochre sky heralded more snow. He felt very tired.

'I'm grateful for your concern, Paul, but Amy has more than enough on her plate at the moment. Couldn't this wait?'

'Not really.' Paul's voice betrayed his exasperation. 'Judith and I are more than willing to shoulder the extra burden. We're here to help, not hinder. The best thing we could do for you would be to take over the day-to-day running and introduce more money-making ideas ... you and Amy wouldn't have to be concerned with it at all. Profits would be up. Everyone would benefit. You and Amy – Stella and Jim – the children …'

'And you and Judith,' Bob said quietly.

'Well, yes, of course. But for a very small outlay we could see profits doubling, trebling even.'

Bob surveyed his brother-in-law. At that moment, letting someone else take over the running of Lavender Cabs was a very attractive proposition. It would give him and Amy some precious time together, and the business would still be making money.

Paul sensed victory. 'Naturally we'd have to sound out Stella and Jim about any changes, I realise that.' He sat back in his chair. 'I'm so glad you can see that the suggestions are sensible – especially now. I wonder what's taking so long with that tea? The girls have been out in the kitchen for ages …'

Out in the kitchen, the kettle had boiled at least three times. Four cups and saucers stood empty on the tea-tray as Amy and Judith faced each other.

'You always were stubborn,' Judith said dismissively, 'even when we were children. You'd never give in.'

'Not to your tantrums over who had the best hair ribbons, no!' Amy retorted. 'And as far as I can see, nothing's changed. You still want what's mine.'

'For heaven's sake.' Judith sighed. 'This isn't a playground squabble. All I'm trying to do is make things a little easier for you – for you and Bob. And Lavender should be half mine anyway …'

'Let's not go into all that again.' Amy switched the kettle on for the fourth time. 'You've bought your way into this business, by fair means or foul, and –'

'Perfectly fair means.' Judith turned from the window. 'By buying shares from your son – who is surely able to make up his own mind about what he wants to do with his life – to become involved in a business which our parents set up. I don't think I'm being unreasonable.'

'You never did.' Amy's memories of childhood spats were suddenly vivid. 'Of course Matt had a perfect right to dispose of his shares. You and Paul had a right to buy them – but not a God-given right to walk into Lavender Cabs and take over.'

'Oh, I see! Paul and I are good enough to act as skivvies but when we offer you some of our business expertise …'

'Your what?' Amy laughed. 'What business expertise? You and Paul have never been in business in your lives! You've been on a management course and now you think you're the next Richard Branson!'

Judith, who had dispensed with her sheepskin coat and various scarves when she'd entered the kitchen, started to put them all on again.

'There's no point in talking to you if you won't take it seriously. With Bob no more than an invalid, your children looking ready to leave the business in droves, and you clinging on to Mum and Dad's outmoded ideas, I'll be surprised if Lavender is still running this time next year!'

Tossing her exquisitely groomed head, she marched past Amy and into the sitting room.

'Paul, we're not stopping for tea.' Her eyes reached her brother-in-law, and softened. 'I'm pleased to see you home, Bob. Really I am. And I do hope you'll take things easy and get completely better. That's all we want. It's just a pity that your wife is so blinkered that she can't see it.'

Paul got to his feet, leaving Bob sitting bemused by the fire.

'Come on, Paul, we're going next door to talk to Mum and Dad.' She looked pointedly at Amy. 'Maybe they'll be prepared to listen.'

Amy watched them skid their way across the cobbles and returned to the sitting room with a grin.

'She'll have a long, cold wait. Mum and Dad have gone shopping in Oxford! I'm sorry, love. That was just what I wanted to avoid. I hope you sent Paul away with a flea in his ear, too.'

'Not exactly.' He patted the arm of the chair. 'Come and sit down.'

Amy perched on the arm of the chair. 'What do you mean, "not exactly"?'

'Well, to be honest, some of what Paul said made sense. Things have changed, love. Things do – we can't cling on to the past just because it's the way it's always been. There have to be changes.' He took her hand. 'We both know that I'm going to be taking a back seat for quite a while, and if it makes things easier for you –'

'So what have you agreed to?' Amy asked.

'Nothing outrageous, nothing that will change the way Lavender's run. But, honestly, if they're willing to involve themselves in the business more, I don't think we should stop them introducing one or two new ideas ...'

'New ideas?' Amy stood up quickly. '"One or two new ideas" now, while we're vulnerable, will become the major changes they've wanted all along! Really, Bob – what on earth possessed you?'

'Come and sit down again and I'll tell you.' He took her hand again and squeezed her fingers. 'We've always run Lavender. It's always been there, and everything else in our lives has revolved around it. My illness has made me realise that there are more important things.'

'I know,' Amy agreed. 'I feel the same – but I can't let Judith take over.'

'It doesn't have to be Judith.'

'What? What do you mean?'

'Mitch didn't want his shares, remember – and Matt obviously couldn't wait to sell his.' Amy shook her head. 'Megan will probably marry out of the business, and – what are you laughing at?'

'You.' Bob pulled her against him. 'You accuse me of not taking any notice of what's going on in this family – but I think I'm far more observant than you give me credit for!

Mitch didn't want his shares at the time – but that was before Jacey Brennan. And,' he went on quickly, sensing her pending outburst, 'Megan's very involved with Lavender. Far more involved than she is with Peter King.' Amy stared at him. 'What are you saying, Bob Phillips? Are you telling me that –'

'That I want to get out of Lavender altogether and spend the rest of my life living peacefully with the woman I love?' He grinned at her. 'Yes, Amy, I am. Now, tell me what you think of that!'

Chapter Eight
Shock News

Megan tidied her bedroom without enthusiasm. She was very tired. She'd done nothing but work flat-out for three days, ever since her father had come home. She'd felt it was the best thing in the circumstances.

The atmosphere throughout Lavender Cabs was very strange. Her parents kept smiling at each other, Paul and Judith were hardly speaking, Dean and Debbie were very quiet, while Matt and Sally might as well have vanished from the face of the earth.

And now there was Peter.

'I'll be there at three,' he'd said on the phone. 'And don't make excuses this time, Megan. We have to talk.'

It was a quarter to three now. She looked out of her bedroom window. The village was silent under its fresh blanket of snow. Lights blazed from the garage and the office, changing from yellow to blue in the shadows.

This meeting with Peter was something she had dreaded, but she knew it couldn't be put off any longer. It wasn't fair to him.

She closed her bedroom door and walked downstairs.

Two drivers grinned at her as they carefully negotiated the slope from the road to the office. She watched as they collected their passengers from the office, then stepped into the yellow warmth. She had to talk to someone, and Debbie would be there.

'Hi!' Debbie looked up from the reception desk. 'You're

not on duty, are you? I thought it was your afternoon off.'

'I'm not and it is.' Megan smiled at her. 'What are you doing?'

'Oh, it's just a sketch.' Debbie tried to cover the piece of paper in front of her.

'Deb! It's brilliant!' Megan looked at the drawing of the village under its cloak of snow. 'You can really feel the cold – and the way the lights are reflected on the snow is amazing! You really should be at art school – not wasting your time here.'

The sketch surprised her. She had expected Debbie, with her black clothes and rainbow hair, to produce aggressive abstract pictures, not this delicate landscape.

'Actually, I've applied to college in London,' Debbie admitted. 'But don't tell Mum and Dad. I'm not saying anything until I've been accepted. I don't mean to be rude but this –' her hand swept round the office '– isn't for me.'

'I'm not surprised,' Megan laughed. 'Lavender Cabs is an acquired taste, although it's one I've grown up with. It's in my blood – but not yours and Dean's, obviously.'

'Dean's been offered a place in the youth orchestra,' Debbie confided. 'We've agreed to tell Mum and Dad at the same time. Sort of halve the explosion …'

'Or double it!' Megan laughed. 'Oh, I'd love to be a fly on the wall.' She glanced at the clock and her face dropped. 'I've got to go.'

She slithered across the powdery snow and collided with Jacey Brennan, who had just got out of her car.

'Hey!' Jacey grinned. 'Where's the fire?'

'There's no fire but there's likely to be a murder!' Megan giggled. 'When my aunt and uncle find out what their offspring have been up to. Debbie's just cheered me up no end. Mitchell's in the garage, by the way.'

'Well, Luke obviously isn't, otherwise you wouldn't be running in the opposite direction.' Jacey laughed. 'How are things going, anyway?'

'I don't know.' Megan shrugged. 'Since we came back from Warwick and Dad had his accident, Luke and I have hardly spoken on a personal level. I don't know what's happening with my life.'

'You need a night out,' Jacey said, flicking snow from the ends of her scarf. 'Why don't you and Luke come out with me and Mitch tonight? There's karaoke at The Cat and Fiddle.'

Megan shook her head. 'I don't think that's my scene somehow. I've got a voice like a strangulated crow. And I don't know if Luke would like it … I know so little about him.'

'Then it's time you found out.' Jacey stamped her feet as the wind howled across the yard. 'I hope we'll be able to get back on the stock car circuit soon, then you and Luke can have some time together – away from all the prying eyes.'

Megan shivered. 'I'm so confused. I know how I feel about Luke, and I know what he said in Warwick, but so many things have changed since then. And there's still Peter.'

'It must be tough.' Jacey was sympathetic. 'Mitch and I are lucky. At least we've got no complications.'

'My life is one big complication.' Megan laughed. 'That's the trouble with being part of a big family, I suppose.'

'I'd love it.' Jacey pulled a face. 'Oh, there seem to be hundreds of us Brennans, but we don't live together – not like you Phillips. We all pass like ships in the night. At least you all care about each other, and your parents are great, even if your mum doesn't approve of me. They're proper parents, always there, always ready to listen.

'You ought to count your blessings, Meg. At least you've got that … and you always will have.' She turned towards the garage, her long blonde hair swirling about her face. 'I'd give anything to be part of it … Oh, well. Better go and root out Mitch before I turn into a block of ice. And good luck with Peter!'

'Thanks.' Megan turned back towards the bungalow. She

did have a lot to be grateful for – she knew that.

She smiled to herself. Debbie and Jacey – so different – had both cheered her up considerably. And once she'd spoken to Peter maybe – just maybe – she'd know where she was going.

She pulled the door open as soon as she saw Peter's car turn into the yard. She hoped to be able to let him down gently, to tell him that she had simply outgrown their relationship. The last thing she wanted was to hurt him …

Her hands were trembling as he hurried towards her.

'Hi! Come in – it's freezing! There's a fire in here …' She knew she was talking far too quickly as he followed her through the hall to the family sitting room. 'Do you want tea or anything?'

He shook his head and made for the fire, holding his hands out to the flames.

Megan sighed. They had known each other for ever, but right at this moment they were like strangers.

'I know this is difficult.' She swallowed. 'I mean – things like this are never easy. I hope we can say things to each other and stay friends.'

'So do I.' Peter spoke for the first time. 'I'm sorry, Megan. About your dad and everything. There's never going to be a right time for this sort of conversation … so I'll say my piece and then –'

'No. Let me.' She turned away and switched on the standard lamp, casting a warm pool of light throughout the big, cosy room. 'Whatever happens, I want us to stay friends. I really mean that. Dad's illness has made me realise that things change, even when you think they'll stay the same for ever, and that in some situations there's no turning back. I've had to grow up and take stock. And although it's painful …' She faltered. She was going to cry.

He moved away from the fire and sat on the sofa, patting the cushion beside him.

'Meg, I'm so sorry … I had no idea this would happen. I suppose I thought we'd always be together.'

She perched beside him, feeling lost and bewildered. This wasn't how she had expected him to be. She had expected him to be full of bluster and bravado. This wasn't the Peter she knew.

He picked up her hand. 'I always thought we'd be married. Always. All my dreams – the house, promotion at the bank, the rugby dos – I could never see myself sharing them with anyone else.'

'Neither could I.' She blinked back her tears. 'But then, I could never see Dad being too ill to work, or Sally and Matt abandoning the business, or Mum's sister appearing from nowhere –'

'It's just as well we can't see into the future, isn't it?' Peter shrugged. 'I expected you to yell and shout at me. I'm glad you're taking it like this … Who told you? Was it Matt?'

'Told me?' Megan's face was perplexed. 'Matt hasn't told me anything.'

'Oh.' Peter sighed. He was still holding her hand. 'I was sure he would. Still, Appleford is such a tiny place it was bound to get out. I only hope you'll forgive me. I should have told you straightaway …

'I met her at the Blue Boar,' he went on, not looking at her now. 'You know, after the match. At first we just chatted about rugby – her brother plays. Then she came to a couple of the games …'

'Who?' Megan felt as though she was in the middle of a play and had been given the wrong script. 'Peter, who are we talking about?'

'Lauren Daniels.' He met her eyes again. 'Oh, Megan, I'm so sorry – but I love her …'

Megan didn't know whether to laugh or cry, and ended up doing both.

'Peter – are you telling me – I mean, am I being –?'

'Yes.' His voice was low, his face anguished. 'I'm sorry,

113

Megan. But things weren't right between us, I can see that now. I honestly didn't mean it to happen. I wouldn't have dreamed it was possible – but Lauren and I …'

He stopped. Was Megan laughing?

Pulling away from him, she walked to the window. It was snowing again.

He quickly crossed the room and put his hands on her shoulders.

'You're all right, Megan, aren't you? Oh, I wouldn't hurt you for the world, you know that. It's just that this time apart has made me realise how much we've changed. And then … well, meeting Lauren …'

'I'm fine.' Megan bit her lip. 'And, yes, you're right – we were just making each other unhappy.' She gave a little laugh. 'I just imagined that I'd be the one who would say goodbye!'

She turned and looked at him, and he smiled gently at her. They had shared so much and had been happy enough.

'I'll go now.' He kissed her cheek. 'Take care of yourself, Megan.'

'Yes. Of course. You too …' Her voice was a whisper as her feelings threatened to engulf her. She had wanted to finish with Peter, she knew she couldn't stay with him. There were so many things she'd meant to say – and he hadn't given her a chance to say any of them.

Once she heard the roar of his car dwindle into the distance, she walked to the mirror that hung above the fireplace. Her face was pale and her eyes looked huge and woebegone.

She gave herself a tremulous smile. 'Well, Megan Phillips,' she told her reflection, 'this is what it feels like to be jilted …'

'We'll never be straight in time!' Sally gazed round the shop. There were boxes, packing cases, bottles, and jars everywhere. 'It's a mess!'

'An organised mess,' Matt corrected her. 'Gran Phillips and Sam are doing a sterling job in the stockroom, and there are still two days to go before we open. Stop panicking.'

Sally grinned. Sally's Floral Oils was at last a reality. The sign was outside to prove it. Now all they had to do was break the news to Matt's parents that they would be moving out of the Lavender Lane bungalow into their own home next month, and everything would be perfect.

'You've got some lovely stock.' Cicely, her hair tied up in a brightly coloured scarf, emerged from the back of the shop. 'You'll do well, my dear. Aromatherapy's all the rage these days and if you do up that back room into a treatment room, you can offer massages and …'

'Hold your horses, Gran!' Matt laughed. 'Let's get off the ground first, oh, I suppose you think that's a pun considering how you and Sam met …'

'Very funny.' Sam grinned broadly as he appeared from the back. 'I'm beginning to feel as though I'm some sort of guilty secret. Your grandmother hasn't seen fit to mention my presence to the rest of the family yet.'

'It's hardly been the right time, has it?' Cicely said, still smiling, 'what with Bob being so poorly and Amy rushed off her feet. But now things seem to have calmed down a bit, I must get round to it. Maybe we'll invite them round next Sunday.'

'I think you ought to tell them before that.' Sam was unpacking little bottles of lavender and patchouli. 'It's hardly fair to welcome them in, tell them dinner will be in about half an hour, and then say, "Oh, and by the way, this is Sam. He's moved in with me", is it?'

'You make me sound like the scarlet woman everyone thinks I am!' Cicely punched Sam playfully. 'I think you should make it clear to these impressionable children that we have separate rooms.'

'Anyway, we'd better break our news first.' Sally took Matt's hand. 'We really are going to have to tell them pretty soon – they'll want to know what to do with our part of the bungalow.'

'They'll probably give it to Megan,' Matt guessed, 'as soon as she comes to her senses and decides to marry Peter King.'

'Oh, I don't think so ...' Cicely observed. 'No – Peter's quite wrong for Meg.'

'And you think Luke Dolan is acceptable, do you?' Matt frowned.

'Absolutely.' Cicely beamed. 'He's young, handsome, spirited, and adores Megan. He's just what she needs. I hope she realises it ...' She broke off. 'Is that someone at the door?'

Matt tugged at the door and was almost knocked off his feet by the howling gale.

'Goodness!' he exclaimed when he saw his parents standing there. 'You're the last people I expected to see! Come in and see how we're doing.'

Bob and Amy stepped into the chaos, and Matt laughed. 'You look like abominable snowmen! When did this lot start?'

'About ten minutes ago.' Bob brushed snow from his coat. 'It's turning into something of a blizzard.'

Amy shook the snow from her scarf. 'Did I hear your gran's voice? Is she helping – or interfering?'

Bob grinned. 'Both, if I know your mother.'

They made their way through to the shop, both halting in surprise at the sight of Sam, swinging Kimberley above his head, much to her delight.

He put her down and held out his hand. 'You must be Bob and Amy. Cicely's told me all about you.'

Bob and Amy exchanged mystified glances, and Sally giggled.

'Gran! Come out here and make the introductions!' She appraised her father-in-law. 'Well, I must say, you look fighting fit. Are you feeling better?'

116

'On top of the world. Better than I have for years.' He cast another puzzled glance at Sam. 'I feel I should know you …'

Cicely bustled out of the stockroom. 'You might have seen a photo. This is Sam, and it's a long story.'

'But before Gran gets going for the rest of the night – there's something we've got to tell you …' Sally said.

Amy linked her arm through Bob's and smiled at them all.

'For once, you can all wait your turn, because we've got something to tell you.' She squeezed Bob's arm tightly. 'Haven't we?'

'We have.' He grinned. 'And I think you'd all better sit down.'

Amy lifted Kimberley into her arms as the others scrambled for packing cases to sit on.

'Now, are you sitting comfortably?' Bob was grinning. 'Then I'll begin …'

He looked so much better, Amy thought, ten years younger, and the worried, grey look that had been part of him for so long had disappeared.

Sally and Matt looked happier, too.

There had been a time when she had feared for their marriage, but now this little shop, their own business, had brought the sparkle back. Just, she admitted to herself, as Lavender Cabs had to her and Bob all those years ago.

But how would the rest of the family react to what they wanted to do now? And was it really going to be that easy, after so many years?

As though echoing her thoughts, Bob began to speak.

'Your mum and I have been talking, and although we'll have to discuss it with Megan and Mitch and, of course, Gran and Granddad Foster – we've reached a decision about our future. First of all – Matt, would you like our part of the bungalow?'

Matt and Sally exchanged glances.

'Actually, Dad,' Matt said lamely, 'we were going to talk

to you about that. Sally and I have – we're buying a house on the Larkspur estate. We'll be moving out.'

'We would have told you sooner,' Sally joined in quickly, 'but with you being ill and everything ... '

Amy gasped. She hadn't expected this. She shot Bob a worried glance. He'd been counting on Matt and Sally. Would this throw a spanner in the works before they had even started?

But Bob was smiling. 'Well, congratulations. That's fine – yes, I'm delighted for you. You're doing something that I should have done years ago, Matt – putting your wife and family first.'

'I've been happy with Lavender,' Amy protested. 'It's given us stability in an uncertain world, and given the kids the security they needed.'

Bob was laughing now. 'It's given us everything you said, and more. But the art of survival is knowing when to let go and move on. Some people never get the chance – we're lucky, and so are Matt and Sally.'

'But where exactly are you going?' Cicely looked at her son. 'I gather you're retiring from the business, but to do what?'

'Mother!' Bob gave her a mock frown. 'I know patience is not one of your virtues, but just hold your horses. We've still got a lot of thinking to do. Anyway –' he looked at Sam and grinned. 'Haven't you some explaining of your own to do?'

'I think we should do all that later, over a nice meal at The Seven Stars,' Sam replied. 'After all, our news seems pretty small beer in comparison.'

'Right,' Amy said briskly. 'We'll book a table at the pub for Saturday night – Matt, will you ring the others arid organise it? We might as well have everybody together.'

'Does the invite stretch to Aunt Judith and Uncle Paul?' Matt was smiling widely, relieved that his news had gone down so well. 'Are you making them guests of honour?'

Amy shook her head. 'Indeed I am not! The invitation

stretches to immediate family only. And, of course, Sam.'

'What about Mitch and Megan's partners?' Cicely put in. 'Aren't you going to include them?'

'I'd rather not share a table with Jacey Brennan – you know I don't like her. And Megan and Peter would be at daggers drawn ...'

Cicely smiled mischievously. 'You're behind the times, Amy. I don't think Peter's in the picture any more.'

'Really?' Amy was abashed. She knew she hadn't talked properly to Megan for ages, and she felt guilty at the surge of delight Cicely's news had caused. When had Megan had the sense to call off her relationship with Peter? She really was going to have to make time for a proper chat.

'So who does the grapevine have her paired off with now?' she asked.

'Luke Dolan,' Matt said shortly. 'Who would be about as popular at the dinner table as poor Jacey.'

'Luke?' Amy and Bob chorused. 'Surely not!'

'I think you should ask Megan,' Cicely said. 'Don't listen to gossip.'

Matt grinned at her. 'Gran! You're the biggest gossip in Appleford!'

'Maybe,' Cicely acknowledged, 'but I've been on the receiving end, too – and I know how painful it can be, especially when it's not true.'

Bob was shaking his head. 'I think in your case, Mother, it was always true, wasn't it? You'd have been very disappointed if it hadn't been!'

They all laughed, and Amy, looking on, sighed. She was going to miss this.

Sally, sensing her sudden sadness, squeezed her arm.

'Don't have any doubts,' she whispered. 'The world is very small. We'll never be too far away.'

'Heavens!' Amy returned her hug. 'We're not emigrating! We're only going to Devon!'

There was a silence as Amy and Bob looked at each other. This was what they had wanted without being aware of it, and they both knew it. Starpoint, the little coastal village where they had taken holidays, the place where they had dreamed of spending their retirement ...

'Devon,' Bob said softly. 'Yes, we are, aren't we?' He cast a quick look round the shop. 'We'll leave you to your hard work, folks. I think your mother and I have got plans to make.'

Outside, the snow was whirling and dancing, and Amy clung to Bob's arm as they slithered towards the car.

'We're being as reckless as the children!' She grinned, sliding into the driving seat. 'Can we do it, Bob? Just up sticks and go to Starpoint?'

'We can do anything we want!' Bob said, with a carefree note in his voice that she hadn't heard for years. 'Life is too short to have "if onlys" in it. Let's go and tell everyone else before we get cold feet.'

'I've got cold everything else.' Amy laughed, steering the car carefully through the blizzard. 'Who shall we start with?'

'It had better be your mum and dad. After all, they gave us the business in the first place, and they're probably going to be hurt most by this. We'll have to be tactful.'

'If it's tact we're aiming for, you'd better leave it to me, then,' Amy retorted. 'You've never been noted for it.'

They laughed like children as they headed back toward Lavender Lane.

'I don't believe it.' Stella Foster leaned back in her chair and looked across at her husband. 'Well, come on, Jim. Say something.'

Amy and Bob, side by side on the sofa, as they had been since their courting days, were still feeling like children. Amy's father stretched, sighed, and tapped his pipe against the fireplace.

'I can understand what you're saying,' he said slowly. 'I can even understand your reasons. And don't think we won't miss you, because we will. But I don't think you've given it enough thought.'

'We know that.' Amy clutched Bob's hand. 'We're being very impulsive. We haven't even been down to Starpoint to see if there's a suitable property or anything. But I don't see ...'

'No.' Jim Foster held up his hand. 'I don't think you quite understand, my love. I assume you don't want Lavender Cabs to go to Paul and Judith?'

'Definitely not!' Amy shuddered. 'That's why we thought of Mitch and Megan.'

'Exactly.' Jim's face was expressionless. 'And to be able to buy a little place in Starpoint and live comfortably in retirement, you'll need to sell your shares and your home, won't you?'

'Yes.' Bob nodded. 'We've got some savings, but nowhere near enough to finance this, so –'

'And where exactly do you think Megan and Mitchell will be able to find the money to buy you out?'

Bob and Amy looked at each other in dismay. It was so obvious, and they'd never even seen it. Were their dreams destined to come to nothing?

'I don't want to see you go, either, but I also know why you want to.' Stella clasped her hands. 'And I agree that in your position I'd want to do the same thing.' She smiled fondly at them. 'Getting away from the stresses and strains of Lavender, spending precious time together, it's all so important. If we could help you, you know we would, but we simply don't have that sort of money.

'Face it, Amy my dear, if you're really serious about this venture, I think you'll have to consider selling Lavender Cabs to your sister.'

Chapter Nine
Hatching The Plan

The snow fell relentlessly for three days and nights. Appleford was practically cut off from the outside world, and Lavender Cabs had almost ground to an uncharacteristic halt. The garage was deserted.

Jacey Brennan sat on the reception desk, swinging her long legs.

'Spit it out, Meg. What's going on with your family? Everyone has the grumps – even Mitch. Is it the weather or what?'

'I don't think we respond well to enforced inactivity.' Megan doodled on the pad in front of her. 'But there's more to it than that. Mum and Dad want to move away.'

'No!' Jacey's blue eyes were like saucers. 'What, sell up? All of you? To go where?'

'That's just it.' Megan sighed. 'They're going to Starpoint – it's a little village in Devon – or so they say. To retire. We're not.'

'Oh.' Jacey sighed enviously. 'Aren't you lucky? I wish my lot would up sticks and give me some space!'

Despite her misery, Megan giggled. 'You're terrible!'

'No, I'm not, merely truthful. So where's the problem? I'd've thought you didn't have any problems at all – what with Peter going off with Lauren and –' Jacey stopped. 'Sorry, that was insensitive, even for me. I suppose after all these years, you miss him, don't you?'

Megan shook her head. 'Funnily enough, no. It was – oh,

more of a relief than anything. It's like getting better when you've been ill for a long time. You never realise just how awful you felt until afterwards. I'm just glad we parted on friendly terms.'

'Oh, good.' Jacey was grinning again. 'What does Luke have to say about it?'

'I haven't told him.'

'Meg! You're impossible!'

'And what was I supposed to say? 'Hi, Luke. Peter and I are finished, so that leaves the way clear for you'?'

'No!' Jacey laughed. 'But surely you could drop subtle hints?'

'I haven't really seen him. I'm beginning to think I dreamed Warwick.'

'You didn't,' Jacey assured her. 'I was there, and Luke was deadly serious. Oh – I wish there would be a thaw and we could start racing again. We need to get you away from here so that you and Luke can sort yourselves out!'

'I've got a feeling I'll be away from here for good before too long,' Megan said mournfully. 'Because if Mum and Dad do move away, it'll mean Judith and Paul will be in charge – and I'm sure they'll give Mitch and me our marching orders.'

'But you own shares …'

'Not enough. To think that I once imagined if I could sort out Peter I'd be completely happy. I never expected Mum and Dad to do this!'

Suddenly overcome, she jumped to her feet and ran out of the office, nearly colliding with her younger brother, making his way carefully across the frozen snow from the garage.

He looked puzzled as he came into the office. 'Was Meg crying?' He kissed the tip of Jacey's nose. 'What's going on?'

'It's this business with your mum and dad.' She snuggled into his arms. 'She doesn't want to leave Lavender.'

'Neither do I.' He stroked her long blonde hair. 'I wish I'd never given my shares back to Gran and Granddad Foster. And I wish Matt hadn't sold his shares to Paul and Judith. Oh, I wish we could win the lottery – then we'd be able to buy Mum and Dad out and start up on our own.'

'Yeah.' Jacey's eyes sparkled. 'Wouldn't it be great? We could keep the taxis and the garage going like now, and have a proper racing team. Oh, well.' She sighed. 'How do you feel about a bank robbery?'

Megan ploughed her way across to the bungalow. Life had been turned upside down. Matt and Sally had their own home and the shop, her parents wanted to leave Appleford, Peter had fallen in love with someone else, and Cicely was starry-eyed about some American stranger and didn't seem to have time for any of them.

And, she thought bitterly, Paul and Judith were poised to step into her parents' shoes.

'Meg!' Amy was brushing snow from the doorstep. 'Come in for a minute, love. I've just made a pot of tea.'

They sat at the kitchen table. Bob was snoring gently in the rocking-chair beside the stove as Megan looked around the kitchen, her heart sinking.

She couldn't leave here! It had been her home since she was born. Every inch of the bungalow held memories. She simply had to stay.

She looked at her mother over her tea cup. 'I don't know how you can bear to leave this place. It has even more memories for you than it has for me. How can you even think of leaving it?'

'Because your dad is more important to me than any house – any business anything,' Amy told her simply. 'The only other things that matter are you all the family. And you're grown up. You and Mitchell will soon be ploughing your own furrows, like Matt and his family. It's the way it should be. Look forward, Meg – never back.' She sighed and stared at the blanketing white wilderness outside the kitchen window. 'Anyway, I think our dreams have ground to a halt.'

'Why?' Megan felt guilty. Her parents loved each other so very much. It was unfair of her to put her own dreams first. 'I thought –'

'We were being foolish,' Amy said shortly. 'We hadn't thought about raising the money. We just wanted to pass Lavender onto you and Mitch the bungalow would divide up nicely into two homes – and you're both involved in the business. We never thought we'd actually have to sell it. And as I refuse to let Paul and Judith get their hands on it, or sell it to outsiders, that looks like the end of Starpoint. But it was a lovely dream while it lasted.'

Megan reached out and took her mother's hand. '"Don't give up on your dreams", that's what you and Dad have always told me, and I haven't. Not that my dreams were very wild or anything. I just wanted to live here, drive, run the business, fall in love and get married and have a family. Fairly old-fashioned, really.'

'They're wonderful dreams, Meg. They're the dreams that I had years ago and mine all came true.' Amy glanced at her husband, her eyes gentle. 'I don't want to lose him. I want us to grow old and grey together, like Gran and Granddad Foster, or Cicely and her Sam.

'I know how heartbroken Cicely was when Bob's dad died. If she's got a second chance of love and happiness, I only hope she takes it. That's what I want to have with Bob – making the most of every minute together. And if doing that means relinquishing Lavender – then so be it. But we can't do any of it without money …'

'There must be some way round it, surely?'

'Selling up lock, stock, and barrel, yes. But that wouldn't be fair on anyone else.' Amy again stared at the snow beneath the darkening sky, then looked back at her daughter. 'Anyway, enough of my problems. How are your dreams coming along? I was pleased that you and Peter managed to part on such good terms, but – er – Gran Phillips said something about – Luke …?'

'She would!' Megan hid her blushes in pouring more tea.

126

'She shouldn't have!'

'But you do like him?' Amy leaned across the table. 'He's a nice lad, Meg. Hardworking, honest, good fun – and very handsome.'

Megan's blushes increased. 'I know! But he's younger than me, and …'

'What on earth does that matter? Listen, Megan, that's what I've been saying. One thing your dad's illness has taught me is that life is very short and very precious. If you and Luke are happy together, then for goodness sake stick with him, and to hang with what the gossips might say!'

Megan laughed. 'I bet you wouldn't be saying that to Mitchell about Jacey.'

'Ouch!' Amy laughed back. 'Jacey's a completely different matter. She's so wild, so –'

'They're very much in love,' Megan said quietly. 'And you ought to give her more credit. Mum. She cares about the business, about the family, about all of us – not just Mitch. If you got to know her, you'd find out she's a very nice girl.'

Amy's snort of disbelief made them both giggle.

'What have I missed?' Bob opened one eye and stretched lazily.

'Two cups of tea and some girl talk.' Megan went over and kissed him on the forehead. 'You're looking better every day, Dad. Early retirement seems to suit you.'

'A rest cure was all I needed.' Bob hitched himself into a sitting position. 'Anything else was just being foolish … The forecasters reckon we've seen the last of the snow and the thaw will be pretty rapid. We'll soon be back in harness again.'

Megan bit her lip. There had to be something she could do, something they all could do. What was the point of having a huge extended family if they couldn't pool their resources and try to come up with solutions?

Amy handed Bob a cup of tea and looked at her daughter.

'Another one for you?'

'No, thanks, I'm awash as it is!' She smiled at her parents. 'Will you do something for me?'

They nodded immediately, and Megan glowed with love. They hadn't even asked what it was. That was how they had always been for her, and for Matt and Mitchell. Now it had to be their children's turn to repay the favour.

'When the thaw does start, take a few days off and drive down to Starpoint. Just have a little holiday. We'll be fine here. You could have a look around, maybe pop into the estate agents, just to – you know ...'

'We could do with a break,' Amy admitted, 'but I can't see the point of looking at places, Meg. We know we can't afford to move. It would be foolish to think ...'

'Dreams, Mum,' Meg said firmly as she opened the door and the ice-cold air flooded into the cosy kitchen. 'Remember what you've just told me. Always hold on to your dreams ...'

It wasn't the best time to be looking at Starpoint, Amy admitted four days later as she and Bob slithered along the cobbled, hilly streets. But even beneath its messy covering of slush, the village still looked magical.

'I've got enough roses in my cheeks to start a florist's shop,' Bob laughed, catching Amy's hand in his own. 'Bracing, isn't it?'

'Very,' Amy agreed, as the wind whipped up from the sea and blew along the narrow alleyways between the cottages. 'I'm sure Mrs Fountain at the guest-house thinks we're out of our minds.'

'She probably thinks we're illicit lovers!' Bob laughed. 'After all, no normal married couple could want to be taking a holiday here in this weather!'

'It is beautiful, though.' Amy flicked wisps of hair away from her glowing cheeks. 'And that last cottage we looked at ...'

'Was the stuff of dreams,' Bob finished. 'And easily within our price range, if –'

Neither of them finished the sentence. There was no need.

They turned the corner away from the sea, and hurried, heads down, towards the guest-house.

Amy smiled to herself, remembering Judith's reaction.

'You're going where?' She had looked at her in astonishment. 'But it's the middle of winter!'

'Bob needs to recuperate properly, and he can't do that if we're on top of Lavender. It's only for a few days, Judith. I'm sure you and Paul can cope. After all, you've got Mitchell and Megan to help, not to mention Dean and Debbie ...'

Amy almost laughed out loud, thinking about the effect her innocent words had had. Judith had sucked in her breath and glared.

'Yes, well, your children may well be available to help out. Mine, I'm afraid, have tired of living in this backwater ...'

'Really?' Amy had fought to keep her lips from twitching. 'Oh, I'm so sorry. They were shaping up nicely. Er – where have they gone?'

'Dean has decided to study music, and Debbie has enrolled at art school.' Judith had had difficulty forming the words. 'They arranged it without even telling us! Paul and I were speechless!'

For the first time in your lives, Amy had thought gleefully, but had managed to sound solicitous.

'Oh, but that's lovely! You must be so proud of them! They're both very talented.'

'Yes, well, of course ...' Judith had been a little mollified. 'But it still means we'll be short-handed at Lavender. The children were such an integral part of our plan.'

'Maybe you should have asked them first,' Amy had ventured innocently. 'I find it usually works with mine. Still, you'll be able to cope until we get back, I'm sure.'

'Why are you grinning like a Cheshire cat?' Bob asked as they climbed the short flight of steps to the guest-house.

'I was thinking about Judith,' she told him, and he hugged her against him.

'Really? She doesn't usually have that effect!'

Amy chuckled. 'She does when she's a couple of hundred miles away and miffed, and I'm here with you!'

Bob patted her cheek. 'You say the nicest things! Come on, I'll race you for the biggest portion of hot buttered teacakes!'

Just as their parents were indulging themselves in a gloriously rich Devon tea beside Mrs Fountain's crackling fire, Mitch and Megan were gazing at each other with furrowed brows.

'How much have you got in the bank?' Mitchell asked.

Megan was scribbling notes on a pad. 'A couple of thousand.'

'Wow!' Mitchell's eyebrows rose. 'That's a fortune! I doubt if I've got more than a hundred. Where did you get that from?

'Saving, little brother,' Megan mocked. 'After all, I was supposed to be marrying Peter at some point. He encouraged me to start a savings account – oh!' She sat upright. 'And I've still got money in the building society for the house deposit.'

Mitchell grinned. 'How much all together? Enough to buy –?'

'Definitely not. I doubt if we can raise five thousand between us, and we'd need a lot more than that! Even if we scraped up enough for Mum and Dad to buy a place to live, they'd still need an income.' She subsided into gloom again, and Mitch rocked back in his chair.

'It's hopeless, Meg. If we want to take over Lavender between us, we'll not only have to raise the asking price, but also buy out our dear uncle and aunt. At least if Matt had kept his shares, that would have helped. Anyway, I can't see Paul and Judith wanting to relinquish their hold – they fought hard enough to get it.'

'I know. I keep going round and round in circles. I was determined that if we got Mum and Dad out of the way for a few days, we'd be able to present them with some plan once they got back ...' They looked at the pad in front of them. With their modest savings, and the money they could raise from selling every possession they could think of, they were still miles away from a realistic target.

Jacey stuck her head round the door. 'Am I interrupting a high-powered business meeting? Can I come in?'

'Only if you've got a six-figure sum stashed away in your mattress!' Mitchell laughed, then looked beyond her. 'Oh, hi, Luke ...'

Megan looked up, met Luke's eyes and smiled. She knew she was blushing and looked quickly away again.

'We've come to see if we can help.' He pulled up a chair beside her. 'Four heads being better than two.'

Jacey hurled herself on to Mitchell's lap.

'Actually, what we thought was, not only could we help you out with the thinking, we could help you out with the actual running ...'

Megan looked at her and then at Luke. 'You mean you'd be interested in –?'

'Forming a partnership?' Luke grinned. 'Yes, we would. After all, Lavender was going to be my future, too. And as Jacey and Mitch seem to be joined at the hip, why not? I've got a little bit of money that my gran left me ...'

'And I've got my motorbike.' Jacey flicked back her hair. 'I know I won't get what I paid for it, but it's still worth quite a bit.'

'You can't sell that!' Mitch protested. 'It's your pride and joy.'

'It'll raise more than a stock car. And I'll sell whatever I've got if it helps.'

Meg wished her mother was there right at that moment.

She might just change her mind about Jacey Brennan.

'We need proper advice,' Luke said, 'but if we can come up with a business plan – and at least some of the money – I'm sure the bank would give us a loan.' He grinned at Megan. 'It would mean making an appointment to see Peter, of course …'

'Don't!' Megan laughed back, then stopped suddenly. She desperately wanted to curl herself into Luke's arms with the unselfconscious ease that Jacey had with Mitchell.

She looked down at the pad again. 'But, yes, I suppose it is an idea. If I get all the figures together …'

'And I'll be working here, too,' Jacey put in. 'As a partner, I'd only take a share in the profits, not a salary. Dean and Debbie have gone, so if we can only get rid of Paul and Judith …'

Megan started to smile. Maybe, just maybe, they'd be able to do it. She'd definitely make an appointment to see the bank manager – even if it meant working all night to produce the figures.

'OK.' She looked at Mitch. 'Shall we give it a go?'

He nodded. 'Why not?'

Luke leaned forward and touched Megan's arm. 'Could we talk? Privately?'

'Oh, don't mind us. We're just going to make coffee anyway.' Jacey slid from Mitch's lap and dragged him to his feet. 'Aren't we?'

'We are.' Mitch grinned, following her through into the back room where the taxi drivers took their breaks. 'Shout when it's safe for us to come back.'

Waiting until the door was closed, Luke lifted Megan's hand and studied her fingers.

'I didn't mean to sound crass about Peter. I – I haven't wanted to say anything in case you were upset.'

'I'm relieved – just relieved, that's all.' Megan shivered in delight as Luke's fingers laced with hers. 'I didn't know how to tell you. Things have been so awful lately.'

'I know.' He leaned forward and gazed into her eyes. 'But they don't have to be any more, do they? I mean it about the business, you know. I really think the four of us could make a go of it. Jacey's a brilliant mechanic, as well as a driver, and I certainly don't want to leave here – or you …'

Megan turned her head away quickly, knowing she was going to cry, and Luke stroked her hair.

'Listen, Meg. There are a lot of other options, but even if there weren't, I'd like to do something else …'

She looked at him then. It didn't matter if he saw her tears.

'I love you,' he said softly. 'I always have. I – I could sell my flat. It wouldn't raise an awful lot, but it would be something more to add …'

'But where would you live?' She was inches away from him now. 'You can't do that, Luke, not for Lavender.'

'For you,' he said quietly, kissing her. 'I'd do anything I could for you. And I could always move into the bungalow with you.'

'What?' Megan shook her head, but he was laughing.

'Meg, darling, I'm asking you to marry me.'

'Married?' Megan said slowly. 'Us?'

He frowned. 'Have I just made the biggest goof of all time, Meg? I mean, I really thought –'

'Yes,' Megan said quietly.

Luke looked even more perplexed. 'Yes, I have – or yes, you will?'

'Yes, I will!'

With a joyous whoop, he gathered her into his arms and kissed her.

Mitch and Jacey, emerging from the rest room to investigate the commotion, started in amazement.

'Have they just solved the question of finance, do you think?' Mitch whispered, and Jacey shook her head, grinning hugely.

133

'I'd say they've just arrived at a far more important decision. Let's leave them to it for a bit,' she urged, and dragged him out of the room again.

Coming down to earth, still clasped in Luke's arms, Megan smiled.

'Do you realise that we haven't even been out together more than once? We're going to be married, and we haven't even had the courtship yet!'

'We'll do that later.' He stroked her hair away from her face. 'We've got the rest of our lives together to sort out the finer points.' He kissed the tip of her nose. 'And we've done all the important things, haven't we? We've been friends for ages, know everything about each other. There won't be any skeletons leaping out of the cupboard.'

Megan leaned against him. He was right. This was right, absolutely. She'd dated Peter King for years, considered marrying him, yet never once had she felt a fraction of the love and happiness welling inside her now.

'We don't have to get married quickly,' she said into his shoulder. 'Not if –'

'I think we do, actually.' Luke was laughing. 'That is, if I'm going to sell the flat as my contribution to the new Lavender partnership. Unless, of course, we fly in the face of convention.'

'No!' Meg looked up at him and blushed. 'Sell it. Oh, Luke, I do love you.'

She burrowed against him again, wondering fleetingly how her parents would react to the news. She was almost sure they would be delighted, but even if they weren't, nothing on earth was going to stop her marrying Luke.

Jacey's blonde head appeared round the door. 'Is it safe to come out now? And are congratulations in order?'

Megan laughed, still clasped in Luke's arms. 'Yes, and yes!'

Suddenly they were all hugging and kissing each other, and Mitch raised his coffee cup.

'Here's to Luke and Megan – and their future! And to the other new partnership – Lavender Cabs!'

They clinked mugs, giggling, and Jacey swept back her golden hair.

'You're allowed to have your feet off the ground for another few hours, Megan, and then I'm afraid it'll be all down to business. I've phoned the bank. You've got an appointment with Mr Bamford in the morning.'

Megan continued to smile. After this, what could possibly go wrong?

'We'll work all night on the figures.' Mitch perched on the desk. 'And produce a business plan. We won't leave any loopholes, so they won't be able to say no.'

It was a long night. Buoyed up by endless cups of coffee and toasted sandwiches, the four of them added and subtracted, argued and agreed, with Megan's fingers skimming across the computer keyboard and the printer spewing out paper.

At last, they were finished.

'Well.' Megan gathered up the sheets and put them in her briefcase. 'We've got two chances. Keep all your extremities crossed.'

They laughed, and arms linked, tumbled wearily out into the slushy night.

The bank manager's office was austere, designed, Megan thought, to strike terror into the hearts of those who had strayed into the red. She sat dry-mouthed as Mr Bamford leafed through the papers.

Luckily Peter had been nowhere in sight when she'd arrived, although some of his rugby-playing cronies had raised their eyebrows before saying polite good mornings. Megan had beamed back, still not quite believing what had happened.

She and Luke had been reluctant to part last night. They'd talked for ages.

He'd been horrified that she didn't want an engagement ring. When she'd explained that every penny needed to be conserved for the business venture, and that as their engagement was going to be very short a ring would be a frightful expense, he'd lifted her off her feet and told her that she would be wearing his ring before the week was out.

Still smiling at the memory, she raised her eyes to the bank manager. 'Sorry – I didn't quite catch that ...'

She was really going to have to concentrate and stop beaming like a Cheshire cat or Mr Bamford would surely think she was of unsound mind!

'I said,' he repeated, peering over both his half-moons and the little pyramid of his fingers, 'that this is a very interesting proposition. Very interesting. I am, of course, aware of the potential of the business, and its long-standing tradition, and you have all worked extremely hard to present a very workable plan.'

Megan's spirits soared.

'However,' Mr Bamford continued, 'I am a little concerned at the amount of money needed to buy out the current shareholders. Until I've had consultations with the bank's small business advisors, I won't be able to make a definite decision.

'It would, of course, be far more beneficial if your parents intended merely to retire in Appleford and didn't want to take capital from the company to buy a new property. But I do understand the situation, and will give it all due consideration.' He stood up and held out his hand. 'We will be in touch, Miss Phillips, very shortly. Good morning.'

Stepping out into the grey High Street, with piles of slush turning brown against the sides of the road and the wind blowing litter in dancing eddies along the pavement, Megan let out her breath. She'd done all she could. They all had. It was in the lap of the gods now, and – she laughed out loud as she hurried towards the car park – the small business advisors!

'Megan!'

She turned quickly and peered over her shoulder. Please, oh please, she prayed, don't let it be Peter.

It wasn't. Her uncle and aunt, muffled in matching sheepskin coats and cashmere scarves, were waving from the other side of the road.

Megan wondered if she could get away with simply waving back, but she couldn't. They were crossing the road towards her.

'Meg.' Judith pressed her cheek against her niece's. 'How lovely.'

Megan looked at her in some surprise. Was it? And what were Paul and Judith doing in town, anyway? She'd thought they were back at Lavender, ruffling feathers and disrupting the smooth running of the business.

'We were just going for coffee,' Paul announced. 'Would you like to join us?'

'Er – well,' Megan faltered, 'I shouldn't really. I ought to be getting back. Who's running the office?'

'That Jacey girl,' Judith said. 'Although what good she'll be, I don't know. She looked half asleep, and I'd say she hadn't been home last night. I'm pretty sure she emerged from Mitch's flat. Just because your parents are away … I shall have something to say to them when they get home.'

Goodness, Judith really was poisonous!

'Mitch and Jacey are adults,' Megan said quickly. 'I'm sure Mum and Dad would have no interest in any gossip of that sort.'

'No, no, of course not.' Paul shot a look at his wife. 'Anyway, that's by-the-by. Do come for coffee. Have you been banking the takings?'

Megan nearly laughed. They didn't miss a trick!

'Yes,' she lied easily. 'All right. I'll have a quick coffee – then I really will have to get back.'

'Of course.' Judith linked her arm intimately through Megan's and looked triumphantly at her husband. 'This meeting was certainly fortuitous, Meg, darling, because

137

Uncle Paul and I have something to tell you. But you must promise not to breathe a word of it to anyone else … '

Amy's parents, Stella and Jim, sat side by side in Cicely's kitchen. Sam sat on the opposite side of the table, neatly folding papers and official-looking forms.

'So?' Cicely plonked the teapot in the middle of them. 'What are we going to do with them? You know, Stella, I thought we'd finished with all this anguish about our children years ago!'

'So did I.' Stella reached for a digestive biscuit. 'This reminds me of when we planned their wedding. It only seems five minutes ago, doesn't it? They were young and dotty about each other – and we were agonising over our hats!'

'And now,' Jim put in briskly, 'they're middle-aged and, thankfully, still dotty about each other. And we're great-grandparents, and we still worry about them. So, what's to do?'

Cicely joined them at the table. It was very much the same as planning the wedding, she thought with just a twinge of sadness, but then the man beside her had been Bob's father. Now Sam was here, dear Sam, who had always meant so much to her.

She had been very lucky with David, she knew. He had been the best and kindest of husbands, always fair, loving, and uncritical. If he had had any idea that his young fiancée had momentarily given her heart to another man, he had never once mentioned it.

And now Sam was miraculously back in her life. She had been given a chance to recapture the fleeting happiness of that long-distant summer when he had been a dare-devil pilot and she had been – she smiled to herself – carefree and more than a little wild.

She watched Sam chatting easily with Amy's parents, and wondered where the years had gone.

'So,' Jim was saying, 'that leaves us with the unpalatable

138

fact that the only way we can release enough capital to let Amy and Bob move away is by selling their shares to Judith and Paul – and we all know what Amy's feelings are on that.'

Sam replaced his teacup into the saucer with a clatter.

'I think I may have some sort of a solution.' He reached out and patted Cicely's hand. 'I know Cicely doesn't want to discuss this yet, but I honestly think that we don't have too much time. You see, folks, I'm going to be selling up in the States and moving back here. I've always thought of England as home, even though I've been away from it for the best part of my life. I've got no one left in America except a host of friends. And my heart has always been on this side of the Atlantic Ocean.'

He smiled at Cicely, and Stella and Jim exchanged a glance. They had already discussed this possibility. They both remembered the rumours that had abounded all those years ago – and the scandal that had rocked the village when Cicely, engaged to David, who was going to be a minister, had become a wing-walker on Sam's plane. Now, they were simply delighted that Cicely was happy.

'That's grand news!' Jim pumped Sam's hand. 'And can we expect to hear wedding bells?'

'Goodness, no!' Cicely laughed. 'We haven't had bells at the church here in Appleford for years. They use a recording these days. I'm so glad David isn't around to hear it. That peal was his pride and joy.'

'But you will be getting married?' Stella asked gently. 'I know you've always flown in the face of convention – if you'll excuse the pun, Sam – but really, Cicely, it would cause awful gossip if you –'

'Lived together?' Cicely trilled. 'But that's exactly what we're doing at the moment!'

'With separate rooms, as we've made clear to everyone.' Sam put in. Sometimes he wished Cicely wouldn't tease people so much. 'Don't worry, Stella. We did all our shocking things years ago. We're quite. conventional these days.'

Cicely laughed. 'You speak for yourself!'

'But surely you won't be marrying in a register office, will you?' Jim poured himself another cup of tea. 'They always seem so austere. And with your connections with the church ...'

Cicely and Sam smiled at each other across the table.

'Actually, some register office weddings that I've attended have been absolutely charming,' Cicely said. 'But, no, we won't be making our commitment in one.'

Stella and Jim looked so exasperated that Sam laughed aloud.

'Oh, Cicely! For goodness' sake! Put them out of their misery!'

'Very well. This is all rather hazy of course, because we haven't set any dates, and I certainly don't want you to breathe a word of it to Bob and Amy. We want to tell them ourselves.'

'Cicely!' Stella was getting impatient.

'Well, we thought that as there are all sorts of places authorised to carry out civil wedding ceremonies, it might be a rather nice idea to make our commitment to each other at Milton St John.'

Jim nearly choked on his biscuit.

'The old airfield? You can't get married on an airfield!'

Sam grinned. 'We can, you know. Oh, not actually on the field itself, because it's still used for training flights and the vintage air club. But Milton St John House is one of the places where weddings can now take place. They've even agreed to let us have a flight afterwards in the old Boeing Stearman – sadly, not the one I used to fly with Cicely, but it's pretty close. We thought it was perfect.'

'Goodness me!' Stella pursed her lips. 'Whatever next?'

'I'm sure that if Mitch and Jacey ever decide to marry they'll be thrilled to do it on a stock car circuit!' Cicely laughed, pouring more tea all round, secretly delighted that she could still shock people. 'So why shouldn't we do it at the place where we met?'

'But you're still known in the village as the vicar's wife,' Jim insisted. 'What about the church?'

'All taken care of.' Cicely closed her hand over Sam's again. 'We're going to have a church blessing immediately afterwards. Everyone will be at the church. We want the actual marriage to be very private, but we want everyone to be at the blessing. Won't it be lovely?'

'Lovely,' Stella echoed faintly, wondering what on earth Amy and Bob would have to say. 'And when is all this to be?'

'We haven't set a date yet, because obviously Sam has to go back to America and finalise things, but we're hoping sometime in May or June. Plenty of time for you to buy a hat,' she added, her eyes twinkling.

Stella perked up considerably. Her collection of hats for every occasion might be a standing joke in the family, but the excuse to buy another was always welcome.

'Before you two start a never-ending discussion on clothes for the big day,' Jim interrupted quickly, 'can I offer my sincerest congratulations? And I really hate to drag you back to more mundane matters – but we were supposed to be discussing the future of Lavender Cabs –'

The other three looked at him shamefacedly.

'Bob and Amy will be back tomorrow,' Jim went on, 'and we really should have something to tell them. Sam what was it you were going to say?'

'Just that when I've tied up things in the States, I'll have a certain amount of income to invest. Cicely and I will have more than enough for our future, and I can't think of anything I'd like better than to be able.to help my new family with the residue.'

Stella and Jim exchanged glances. They had mixed feelings. They knew that for the sake of Bob's health and Amy's happiness, it was imperative that they should retire from the business but even so ... the firm had been in the family for a long time. They weren't absolutely sure they wanted to have Sam in overall charge.

But what other choice was there?

Only the one that they both knew Amy would never accept – selling out to her sister and brother-in-law.

Sam, sensing their reluctance, tapped the papers in front of him.

'I don't think I've explained things very well. I don't want to become a sleeping partner – or even a sleeping owner – of Lavender Cabs. We'll be too busy for that – we're gonna buy a biplane and join the vintage aviators!' He smiled. 'No, what Cicely and I are planning to do is share the money out between the children.'

'Oh!' Stella leaned forward. 'The children? What a wonderful idea – and how very generous!'

'Well, they'll get it after we're gone anyway, so it seems more sensible to let them have it now,' Cicely remarked. 'Obviously I've already helped Matt and Sally set up Floral Oils, so their share would be smaller, but there will be some for baby Kim. And Bob and Amy will have a larger share than Mitch or Megan. We've seen my solicitor and he's working on the final sums now. There will certainly be enough for Bob and Amy to retire on – but not, I fear, quite enough for Megan and Mitch to buy out Paul and Judith as well.'

'So – that means Lavender Cabs will stay in the family into the next generation!' Jim leaned back, smiling broadly. 'And, of course, when Stella and I are gone, our shares –'

'– will have to be divided between Amy and Judith,' Stella said dryly, 'unless we change our will. No – don't let's even think about that. We've all got years of living to do yet! And if Cicely can join the aero club I think I might consider scuba diving!'

'Or stock car racing?' Jim put in mischievously. 'I'm sure the children would be delighted to give you lessons!'

'Stop!' Cicely cried. 'Or when Bob and Amy are back I'll

be accused of leading you astray! We'll just leave the finer points to the solicitors and the accountants, shall we? And hope Paul and Judith take the hint and ride off into the sunset.'

'What a pleasant thought.' Sam was beaming broadly. 'Now, who wants more tea?'

Chapter Ten
Leaving Our Dreams Behind

'Time to go home,' Amy said wistfully. 'And I don't want to. But I shouldn't be feeling like this, should I?'

'Why not?' Bob put his arm round her shoulders. 'I do.'

They were standing against the harbour wall at Starpoint, staring out across the grey-blue mottled water, watching the fishing boats taking a well-earned rest against the quayside, while gulls swooped and screamed over the harbour mouth.

It was a gentle day after so much freezing weather, a day when the sky looked as though it had been washed once too often, and the sun was but a pale imitation of its usual fiery glory. A day to remind everyone that spring really was just around the corner, and that soon the hilly cobbled streets would be filled with holidaymakers.

'That cottage, Windwhistle ...' Amy snuggled against Bob's coat sleeve and repeated the name. She could almost see herself writing it at the top of letters home to the family in Appleford – 'Windwhistle, Cove Lane, Starpoint, Devon.' She sighed. 'It really is perfect, isn't it?'

Bob nodded. 'And vacant possession. It really seemed like home – which is odd, after "home" for all our lives being bound up with so many other people. Are we getting selfish in our old age, do you think?'

'No.' Amy stood on tip-toe and kissed his cheek. 'We're starting all over again. We're doing this the wrong way round, aren't we? This is how most young couples start off, a new home, just the two of them. Away from the family ...'

She stared out across the bay again and bit her lip. They weren't, though, were they? Because they couldn't.

Lavender Lane and all their responsibilities were preventing them from turning the dream into reality.

Amy shook herself. 'Oh, I'm an ungrateful so-and-so. After all, Lavender Cabs has given us so much. I shouldn't resent the very thing that has given us and our children security and stability …'

'But you do.' Bob held her hand tightly. 'And so do I. I don't like myself for it, either. It's just that I've never wanted anything more than this in my whole life.'

'Neither have I,' Amy said fiercely. 'I can almost visualise Windwhistle furnished with our bits and pieces – the dining-table would look perfect by the French doors. Summer evenings with that lovely garden full of jasmine and honeysuckle, and the children coming to stay – and Kim playing on the beach.'

'And we've got to go back and forget all about it.' Bob tightened his grip on her hand and turned her to face him. 'Unless –'

'I can't do it.' She shook her head. 'It wouldn't be fair to Megan or Mitchell. I couldn't sell out to Paul and Judith. Could you?'

They started to walk back towards the guest-house. Their cases had been packed after breakfast and stowed in the boot of the car, to enable them to spend as much of this last day as possible in Starpoint.

'Right now, yes, I could.' Bob didn't meet her eyes. 'I feel inclined to let Mitch and Meg take their chances. They're young – and they'd probably cope with it.'

'But what about Mum and Dad?' Amy said fiercely. 'They don't want Lavender to change! They'd hate it if it turned into a leisure complex.'

Bob stopped and pulled Amy round to face him. She was still so pretty, and these few days away from the stresses of Lavender Lane had eased away the tired lines from her face and brought the sparkle back to her eyes.

'Don't you think we should stop thinking about all of them for once? Your parents, my mother, our children? Why don't we think about us?'

'I do!' Amy protested. 'But never first. I've never been able to afford that luxury! That's the way it is, isn't it? You're part of a family – and you never have time to be you!'

'Except here, for these few days.'

'Oh, yes.' She linked her arm through his and started walking again. 'This has been wonderful. Why does it seem so selfish to be happy away from them all, Bob, when I love them all so much?'

'It's not selfish at all. They're living their own lives – and I think what we've tried to do is to make them want to live ours.' He paused for a moment, knowing that he would have to choose his next words very carefully. 'Because that's what we did. We carried on with Lavender Cabs and the bungalow in exactly the same way as Stella and Jim, because that's what we wanted at the time.

'But things have changed; we've changed. I think it's unreasonable to expect our children – and theirs – to do things exactly as we did just because it's the way our parents did it. It's not the way of the world, Amy. Things move on. And I think we should.'

'But Mum and Dad ...' She sighed. 'They practically gave us the business. It would be so ungrateful to just chuck it back, wouldn't it?'

'We're not chucking it anywhere!' Bob laughed at her woebegone face. 'We're selling it to your sister, which is hardly selling out to a stranger, and allowing our children to have a share in running it, too. It couldn't be more in the family than that, could it?'

'I suppose not. But Mum and Dad will go mad.'

'Then let them.' Bob was firm. 'Let them decide what Paul and Judith should do with it. Amy, you've always been there for your parents, for the kids, and for me. And I've

147

always felt it was in that order – with Lavender coming before any of us. Now, if you agree to sell out to Judith and Paul, we'll have enough money for Windwhistle. If we keep a few shares, it'll give us some income. We've got savings. We could manage. We'd have everything we'll ever need. Amy, please do this for me ...'

Her eyes filled with tears, and she remembered how she had felt when he had the accident. She had promised him on that appallingly lonely night in the hospital when she had thought he might die that she would do anything. If working for Lavender took him away from her, there would be no point in anything. Bob was the only person who really mattered ...

She dashed away the tears and swallowed.

'OK. Let's go back to the guest-house and ask Mrs Fountain if we can stay for one more night. We'll talk to the estate agent again. Let's make an appointment with the bank here ... And we'll ring home and tell Megan that we're staying another day. Let's do it!' Suddenly her words were tumbling over themselves in her excitement. She had never felt so young, so carefree.

With a whoop, Bob scooped her off her feet and swung her round. An elderly couple passing tutted loudly.

'Youngsters! No sense of decorum!'

Giggling together, Bob and Amy hurried back up the hill. It didn't matter if they delayed their return for another day, Amy thought, because nothing ever really happened in Appleford – or at Lavender Cabs. It would be exactly the same when they got back, today, tomorrow, next week.

After all, what could possibly have changed?

The sun was shining with almost summer brightness when Bob and Amy drove into Lavender's yard. Amy looked at the bungalow, the garage, the taxis, and her heart sank.

'Tell me I'm wicked not to want to be here.' She looked across at Bob as she braked. 'Tell me this is my home. Tell me that Starpoint is still a crazy dream – and that selling my shares to Paul and Judith is the stupidest thing I could be doing.'

'No!' Bob looked tired after the journey. 'That's exactly how I feel, too. As soon as we've unloaded the car, we'll see Stella and Jim and tell them what we're doing, then the kids. After that, everything will be easy.'

Amy doubted it as she lugged the cases from the boot, refusing Bob's offer of help and sending him indoors to make the inevitable welcome-home pot of tea. Momentous changes like these were never easy – and when they involved her sister, she was sure they would be pretty difficult.

'Mum!' Megan appeared from the office, her smile wide. 'Did you have a lovely time? What have you been doing?'

Amy dropped the cases and enveloped her in a hug.

'We had a wonderful time, thank you. But it's what you've been doing that seems more relevant. Look at you, Meg! You're beaming from ear to ear! What on earth's been going on?'

'Loads.' Megan picked up one of the cases. 'More than you'd ever guess! I can't wait to tell you!'

Bob poured out the tea while Meg and Amy both talked at the same time. He smiled to himself. The peace and tranquillity of the last few days were definitely over.

'So,' Amy's voice rose above her daughter's, 'we've come to a decision. We're going to move to Starpoint, permanently. We've found a cottage, it's called Windwhistle, Meg, and it's perfect … but – and this is a big but to be able to buy it we're going to have to sell our shares to –'

'And he asked me to marry him and I said yes!'

They looked at each other. Bob put the pot on the table with a clatter. 'Who? Good Lord, Meg. You're not going to marry Peter King?'

'No, Dad!' Meg wound her arms around his neck. 'If only you'd listen!'

'It'd be easier to listen if you weren't both talking at

once,' Bob grumbled, smiling. 'Who exactly are you marrying?'

'Luke.' Meg sighed with pure happiness. 'Isn't that wonderful?'

'Wonderful,' Bob and Amy echoed together, bemused.

'We're not going to have a proper engagement or anything – we're just going to get married, because of Lavender, and –'

'Meg!' Amy shook her head. 'We've only been gone a few days. You weren't actually going out with Luke when we left, were you? And what do you mean, because of Lavender?'

'Well,' Megan pulled out a chair and poured tea into three cups, then paused and looked at them 'What did you mean about selling your shares and moving permanently? That's wonderful – oh, I mean, we'll miss you, but it's what we wanted for you – but have you got a buyer? Because –'

'Enough!' Bob roared at them both. 'One story at a time, please. Meg, forget what your mother said – we'll discuss it later. Just tell us about you and Luke Dolan …'

Megan did. It took three cups of tea, but no one interrupted her. When she'd finished, Bob and Amy were both gazing at her with brimming eyes.

'You're pleased, aren't you? You do like him?'

'Of course we like him.' Bob was beaming from ear to ear. 'He's perfect for you, Meg. I'm absolutely delighted …'

'So am I,' Amy said, squeezing Meg's hands. 'So when's the wedding going to be?'

'Soon.' Meg grinned again. 'Luke's selling his flat, you see, so he'll be moving into my part of Lavender – and we won't do that without getting married, of course. Jacey and Mitch will be moving in together, but they're different.'

Amy and Bob exchanged glances. Anything they had to say on that score could definitely wait until later – and would no doubt fall on deaf ears. Mitchell and Jacey were hardly the most conventional of couples.

Reluctantly Amy smiled. Whatever misgivings she'd had about Jacey Brennan were unimportant now. Bob had made her see that she couldn't live the children's lives for them, and two out of three respectably married wasn't a bad average.

She frowned. 'But why are you all moving into Lavender? I mean, we hadn't decided to move to Starpoint until a couple of days ago, so how did you know …?'

'We didn't,' Meg acknowledged. 'But we'd guessed. We decided that if we could buy you out and run the business between the four of us, you'd have enough money to retire on. So we went to the bank.' She looked at her parents triumphantly. 'And they're seriously considering our proposals!'

'You mean, Lavender would belong to you and Mitch? That you'd carry on the family tradition?' Amy's eyes began to shine as she understood. 'Oh, that's wonderful! Absolutely wonderful. What brilliant, thoughtful children we've reared. I think we deserve a pat on the back!'

'So do I! And with Luke and Jacey it'll be a third-generation business – maybe even a fourth.' Megan laughed. 'Just what you always dreamed of.'

'Hold on a second.' Bob stopped laughing and laid his hands on the table. 'It won't be just the four of you, will it? There're Paul and Judith to consider, too.'

'That's right.' Amy nodded. 'I mean, whatever you four financial whizzkids have come up with, I can't see it being enough to buy out Judith and Paul. And if Dad and I are going to raise the money for Windwhistle, I'm going to have to sell my shares …'

'Actually, I'm not sure they're going to want them,' Megan said.

'What?' Amy gasped. 'But they've got to buy them! We can't go ahead unless they do! They've been angling for nothing else ever since they arrived in Appleford. What on earth are they playing at?'

'I honestly don't know. I saw Aunt Judith and Uncle Paul on the day I went to the bank, and they confused me completely. They said I'd have to be sworn to secrecy – and then burbled on for hours and told me precisely nothing!'

'Typical,' Bob muttered. 'If anyone's going to throw a spanner in the works, it'll be those two.' He sighed heavily. 'Well, that's that then. If they don't buy the shares we're right back at square one.'

'Bob.' Amy took her hand in his. 'Calm down. Don't let them upset you. After all, we don't know what their plans are, do we?'

'Whatever they are, they probably won't benefit us. Judith has never had family loyalties at the forefront of any of her plans! Perhaps we should talk to your parents. They might know something.'

'They might.' Amy frowned. 'Paul and Judith are obviously playing some devious game.' She looked at her husband with a smile. 'You never know, they might have won the lottery and be planning to buy out the whole shebang! They could be going to offer us millions.'

Bob grinned. 'And pigs might fly! We haven't even got the sand out of our shoes yet, and your dear sister is already making waves.'

He looked across at Megan and his grin softened. 'I can see you're itching to bounce back to the garage and glue yourself to Luke. Run along and invite him over for a drink. We ought to be celebrating your almost-engagement in some sort of style.'

Megan leapt to her feet and hugged them both.

'Don't worry about anything. I'm sure it'll all work out in the end. After all, everything else is so perfect – Aunt Judith and Uncle Paul simply can't spoil it, can they?'

In Cicely's cottage, Mitch looked at the cheque in his hand and thought he was going to faint.

'Good heavens, boy!' Cicely chuckled at him. 'It's only

money!'

'It's a fortune,' Mitch said quietly. 'It's like winning the lottery.'

Sam grinned. 'Hardly. There's an equal amount for Meg, and a smaller one for Matt, because, of course, Cicely has already invested in Sally's shop. We thought you could probably do with yours now.'

Impulsively Mitch threw his arms round them.

'I'll never, never be able to thank you enough!'

'Yes, you will.' Sam beamed fondly at the young man who reminded him so much of David, his friend and his beloved Cicely's first husband. 'Put it to good use in the business, that's all the thanks we need. You deserve it. I know you'll use it well.'

'There is one proviso,' Cicely said gravely, 'and without that I simply won't allow the cheque to be cleared.'

'What?' Mitch, knowing his grandmother, grinned. 'Are you acting on Mum and Dad's behalf? Do you want me to announce immediate wedding plans too?'

'Of course not!' Cicely sniffed. 'You should know me better than that. Oh, I'm sure you and young Jacey will be Mr and Mrs at some stage, but that's none of my business or anyone else's. No, I want something much more exciting.'

The men exchanged mystified glances. Cicely's eyes were twinkling.

'I want you and young Jacey to use some of that money to put together the best cars the stock circuit has ever seen. I want you both to win everything you possibly can next season – and I want a ringside seat for every race!'

'Oh, Gran!' Mitch hugged her again. 'I do love you!'

Sam stood up and went to fetch glasses from the sideboard.

'We'll just wait for Luke and Meg to come back from the bank, and then I'll pour the champagne. This is certainly a day for celebration.'

153

As Mitch helped him polish the champagne flutes, Cicely sat back in her chair and closed her eyes.

Be happy for me, David, she said silently. Sam's a good man – and I love him with all my heart. But I love you, too, and always will. You made me so very happy, darling – and Sam is making me happy now.

'Gran?' Mitchell's voice was close to her ear. 'Are you OK? Were you asleep?'

'No.' She smiled, feeling the warmth stealing inside her. 'I was just having a few words with your grandfather.'

'Oh. And did he have a few words back?'

Cicely nodded. 'Oh, yes. He always does.'

'Were they the right ones?'

She was silent for a minute. He was perceptive, this grandson of hers, far more perceptive than any of them gave him credit for. For all his wild ways, Mitch understood more than anyone.

'Yes, Mitch.' She smiled gently at him. 'They were the right ones.'

'I'm glad. Gran.' He glanced at Sam. 'I know you'll both be happy. Luke and Meg have just pulled up outside – we'd better uncork the champers!'

Cicely bustled out to meet the new arrivals, kissing them both expansively and congratulating them on their engagement.

She drew Megan aside. 'Well? How did it go? Did they say yes?'

'To most of it.' Megan gnawed her lower lip. 'They're prepared to back our business plan. Of course, we'll be stuck with Paul and Judith as minor share-holders. But – and it's a huge but – I can't see any way this will release enough money for Mum and Dad to go to Starpoint … and that's what this is all about, isn't it? I really thought we'd got it sussed this time. But we still need so much more money!'

Without a word, Cicely handed Megan her cheque.

'What's this?' the girl asked.

Cicely smiled, her eyes twinkling with laughter.

'An early wedding present, or a retirement gift for your parents – call it what you will, darling, but it's our contribution – mine and Sam's – to whatever we hope will be a successful partnership, personal and professional.'

Glancing at the cheque, Megan gaped at her grandmother with huge eyes.

'But we can't accept this! This is more money than I've ever seen in my life!'

'You can.' Sam came through from the sitting room and pushed a champagne glass into Megan's shaking hand. 'And you will. Cicely and I will be combining our resources from now on. The sale of my assets will mean we can live comfortably for however many years the Good Lord gives us, so this is our insurance for the future. Investing in you youngsters. Now, come on through and introduce us properly to your young man ...'

The afternoon flew by as they were joined by Jacey, and Gran and Granddad Foster.

Stella and Jim, normally undemonstrative, were so relieved by what Cicely had done that they both hugged her at once.

'Goodness!' Cicely giggled. 'I feel quite squiffy. So, let's have a recap, shall we? Judith will still keep her sticky fingers in Lavender's pie, albeit in a small way. But Amy and Bob can decamp to Starpoint as soon as they like, and Lavender Lane will shortly belong to four of the nicest young people it has been my privilege to know. And Sally, Matt, and Kimberley are snug in their own house, running their own business. Who says life is rotten?'

'I have in the past.' Stella smiled sleepily through her champagne. 'But it's days like today that make all the sad and unhappy times fall into perspective ...'

Jim grinned at his wife. 'Don't let's have any more of

that, Stell. You're coming over all philosophical! I must admit, though, it's nice to know we old 'uns haven't just been turned out to pasture.' He wagged his head towards the four youngsters. 'We'll be around to keep an eye on you, you know, even if your parents aren't!'

'Jim!' Stella admonished. 'They won't want us interfering!'

'Oh, we will. Gran.' Megan managed to tear herself away from Luke long enough to plant a kiss on the top of Stella's head. 'All the time. We'll be running to you for advice and help –'

'And food!' Jacey laughed. 'Cooking is not my strong point!'

'Done!' Stella's eyes gleamed at the thought of feeding four hungry youngsters at the end of a long day. 'It'll be just like the old days, when your mother and Judith were younger and invited their friends for meals.'

'Oughtn't Amy and Bob to be here?' Jacey wriggled her long legs more comfortably on Mitch's lap. 'Shouldn't they be joining in, too?'

'They were asleep when we called in,' Meg said. 'Either side of the fire, books about Devon on their laps, dreaming of country lanes and cream teas.'

They all laughed, and Cicely sat forward.

'Anyway, we're having the family get-together on Saturday at The Seven Stars, aren't we? We'll have a proper celebration then. We can all share our news and plans for the future – and drink the place dry!'

'That won't be difficult.' Sam eyed the empty champagne bottles ruefully. 'And we'll have to break the news to Bob and Amy then, anyway, won't we?'

Cicely's forehead puckered. 'What news?'

'I think,' Sam said, 'in all the excitement, it might just have slipped your mind to tell your son that you're getting married …'

Chapter Eleven
Wedding Fever!

Walking into The Seven Stars was warm and cosy after the sharp shower of evening rain and a blustery wind.

'That was an April shower with a vengeance!' Matt helped Sally struggle out of her coat. 'And I thought spring had come at last.'

Sally laughed. 'I needed it to wake me up. I never thought running my own business would be so exhausting. I can't see any of the others – we must be the first. Shall we go and grab our table – or do you fancy a drink first?'

'A drink.' He steered her towards the bar. 'It's ages since we've been able to do this. I hope Kim settles down all right with the babysitter. You did leave the number here in case there was a problem?'

'Yes!' Sally laughed at him. 'But there won't be. Kim will be fine. And put your wallet away – this is going to be my treat. I've been wanting to do this for as long as I can remember.' She grinned across at the barman. 'Two glasses of white wine, please.'

Matt squeezed her arm. 'You really are happy, aren't you?'

She nodded and handed him his glass, and solemnly they toasted the future.

Matt leaned forward and kissed the tip of her nose.

'I love you, and I'm very proud of you.'

Sally returned the kiss. There had been times in their marriage when she would never have dreamed they would be this contented. But now, having distanced themselves from Lavender, from the close confines of the family, they had rekindled their love.

They were still sitting smiling at each other, fingers linked, when the rest of the party arrived.

'Good heavens!' Matt exclaimed in mock surprise. 'Have we invited the whole town?'

Mitch grinned. 'The Phillips clan is commandeering the restaurant!'

Stella emerged from behind Mitch to kiss Sally. 'Don't forget the Fosters!'

'With the regrettable absence of dear Paul and Judith, who sadly had a prior engagement ...' Cicely beamed, and everyone laughed.

Mitch and Megan exchanged glances. They could do without Judith and Paul tonight – they were going to see enough of them in the future.

Bob looked round his extended family with pride as he raised his glass.

'Here's to the Phillipses and the Fosters! Have they got a table big enough, do you think?'

They had. The manager of The Seven Stars ushered them through to the oak-beamed dining room, where four tables had been pushed together and covered with a vast white cloth set with gleaming cutlery and vases of flowers.

'Freesias!' Amy said in delight. 'My favourites. They smell so gorgeous with the log fire, don't they?'

Bob leaned over, took three pale gold freesias from the vase, and handed them to Amy.

'A corsage, Madam.'

'Cool!' Jacey said in admiration, gazing at Mitch. 'I hope you'll be that romantic when we're their age!'

'Of course he will.' Cicely chuckled as they took their places. 'After all, he's my grandson. We're very romantic on our side of the family.'

'We Fosters aren't so dusty, either,' Jim said, not wanting to be outdone.

Amy sat back in her chair, ostensibly studying the menu, but looking at her family with love. It was simply wonderful to have everyone together like this. There was so much laughter, so much happiness. It would be times like this that she'd remember once they were in Devon.

Bob leaned across. 'And they'll all still be here, Amy. In fact, they'll probably all be with us for so many holidays that we'll have to draw up a rota!'

She smiled gratefully. 'You were reading my mind! Oh, I'm so pleased we've got Windwhistle. That we'll be moving to Starpoint. It's just that I know I'll miss them.'

'Of course you will.' Bob touched her cheek. 'So will I. But we've done a grand job … Look at them!'

Sally and Matt were laughing together over the menu. Mitch and Jacey, as always, were teasing each other.

Amy still wasn't completely at ease with Jacey Brennan, although she had to admit she looked very pretty tonight. Her long blonde hair was secured in a thick single plait, and she'd abandoned her jeans in favour of a dark green velvet dress.

Mind, she still had faint traces of grease under her pearl-pink fingernails, Amy noticed with a fondness that surprised her. She and Mitch were obviously made for one another …

And Luke and Megan? Amy's eyes filled as she watched them. Luke and Megan were like her and Bob all over again. They'd still be madly in love thirty years on, she knew. Their heads were close together, the menu ignored, their glasses of wine untouched.

'It's still just like a dream,' Megan was saying softly. 'I still think I'll wake up and find none of this has really happened.'

'I know.' Luke traced patterns on the back of her hand. 'I'm still in a daze myself. I don't know if I'm on my head or my heels half the time. Still, I've got a definite offer on my flat, the bank have OK'd the business plan, your parents have bought their cottage – we know all those things are real. There's just one thing left.'

'There is?' Megan frowned slightly. 'I can't think of anything else.'

'It's this.' He produced a tiny royal blue velvet box. 'I promised you a ring. I know we may be having the shortest engagement on record, but I still want you to have this ...'

She opened the box and gasped at the sight of the delicate band of cream and grey seed pearls nestling in the velvet.

'It's beautiful!' she breathed. 'But you can't afford it. I mean – oh, I don't want to sound ungrateful – it's lovely, but ...'

Laughing, Luke dabbed at her tears with a napkin, and as the rest of the family watched, carefully pushed the ring on to her finger.

'Don't worry, it really didn't cost very much. It's just a symbol. Oh, Meg, I love you so much ...'

He kissed her as the rest of the table erupted into a wave of clapping and congratulations. Suddenly everyone was laughing and crying and admiring the ring all at the same time.

The entire dining room had stopped eating and was watching with interest, and as soon as they realised what was happening, began calling out their best wishes.

'Champagne!' Sam said. 'We'll have to have champagne now. I know we were going to wait until later, but we can't let this moment pass.'

Cicely, for once completely overcome, was wiping her eyes.

'It's not often I can be accused of being lost for words.' She smiled through the tears. 'But I honestly don't know what to say. I can't ever remember more celebrations in one go. We'll have to have champagne with the starters, whether it's proper or not!'

Bob grinned across the table at her. 'Since when have you been a stickler for convention, Mother? I've known you eat shepherd's pie for breakfast and cornflakes for supper! Champagne with a starter seems reasonably normal!'

As they all laughed, champagne was fetched, and flutes, sparkling in the firelight, were raised.

'To Megan and Luke!' rang the toast through The Seven Stars.

'And have you actually set a date for your wedding?' Cicely called to them.

Luke and Megan looked at each other and smiled.

'We were going to tell you tonight. It's in three weeks' time – the first Saturday in May,' Megan announced, then, as her grandmother started laughing, added, 'What's the matter, Gran?'

Cicely shook her head, chuckling.

'So is ours,' said Sam quietly.

Lavender Lane had never seen such happy chaos. Amy, hopping around with one shoe on and the other dangling from her hand, was trying to fasten her earrings and Bob's button-hole at the same time.

'I knew this would never work!' she exclaimed, dropping her lone shoe in exasperation. 'Only our family could possibly be having two weddings on the same day!'

Bob kissed her forehead as she hovered in front of him, still wrestling with the rosebud and fern.

'At least I haven't got to give away two brides!' he joked. 'Thank goodness we managed to talk Mother out of that one!'

Amy giggled and patted the pin. 'There, you look perfect.'

'And you look sensational!' He laughed, admiring her chic suit. 'Far too young and pretty to be a grandmother – and when you get that hat on you'll knock everyone for six! I could marry you all over again!' He folded her close to him. 'I'm very happy. Very proud. And –' He paused.

'A teeny bit sad?' Amy muttered into his shoulder. 'I know. So many things have changed, haven't they? Think

161

back to a year ago.'

He laughed, and kissed her hair.

'We wouldn't have imagined this in our wildest dreams. Matt and Sally with their own house. Mitch and Jacey living here. Megan marrying Luke. Or my mother marrying anyone! But they're all happy things, love. Especially …'

'Us!' Amy said emphatically. 'That's the happiest bit of all, really. Windwhistle is ours at last, thanks to Cicely and Sam and our children. In two weeks' time we'll be sitting by those French doors, catching glimpses of the sea through the pine trees, never having to worry about another customer or breakdown for the rest of our lives …'

The words hung between them. The rest of their lives together.

'Mum!' Mitch burst into the room. 'Oh, sorry! Didn't realise you were having a cuddle – everyone seems to be doing it today.'

'It's OK.' Bob laughed. 'What's the problem?'

'It's this cravat!' Mitch produced a crumpled ball of silk. 'It won't do what I want it to. I'm used to jeans and sweatshirts – I can't get to grips with this at all!'

Amy finished fastening her earrings, reclaimed her errant shoe, and smiled.

'Here, let me. I always used to have to do your school ties, remember?'

She stood on tiptoe and fastened the cravat, then stepped back with a nod of pride.

'You look wonderful, Mitch. You'll be the handsomest best man in Appleford's history. Now, stay here with your dad and have a glass of something while I go and see Meg.'

Stepping outside into a perfect May morning, Amy paused and lifted her face to the sun. She wanted to savour this moment. For the rest of the day she would be swept along in the mayhem, but now she needed a few moments alone to take stock.

She wondered how long it would take to adjust to the

ambling pace of Devon instead of being jerked awake at ungodly hours to oversee a 24/7 business.

She smiled to herself. It was a problem she was looking forward to; not that she could actually imagine lounging in bed until mid-morning with breakfast on trays and a sheaf of newspapers.

There would be things to do – together. Walks, golf, and bowls, which they'd promised themselves they would learn, visits to the cinema, and all those books they had bought and never found time to read …

She was smiling broadly as she tapped on Megan's door.

Sally, beautiful in her matron of honour's dress of cream and pale green, opened it. Beside her was Kim, wearing a miniature version.

'Just in time!' Sally grinned at her mother-in-law. 'You can give the final verdict. But be prepared for a shock –'

Amy raised her eyebrows. 'She hasn't changed her mind?'

'Far from it!' Sally giggled. 'But your taxi-driving daughter has become a supermodel!'

Eagerly Amy stepped into the bedroom, a chaos of clothes and shoes and make-up, and when her eyes fell on her daughter she was stunned into silence.

'Oh, Meg.' Tears pricked her eyes. She had been with Megan to choose the dress, which had looked glorious, but now … Amy swallowed.

'You look like a princess,' she told her.

Sally sat back on the bed and surveyed her sister-in-law.

The cream silk dress set off Megan's colouring to perfection. The garland of cream rosebuds sat perfectly in her copper hair.

'It took a lot of work to persuade her to wear nail varnish,' she teased, 'not to mention hairspray! But –' she grinned at Jacey '– we managed it in the end.'

'You've done wonders!' Amy shook her head in amazement. 'Has this beautiful lady anything to do with our family?'

'Thanks, Mum.' Megan grinned, gathering folds of the cream silk dress and swishing towards her mother. 'I feel a bit overdone.'

Careful not to crush anything, Amy hugged her, tears welling in her eyes.

'Luke is very, very lucky ...'

Megan smiled. 'So am I. And very happy, and not a bit nervous. Unlike Jacey.' She laughed across the room.

'I've told her that if she's this jittery being a bridesmaid just wait until she and Mitch get married.'

'We'll elope,' Jacey said quickly. 'And tell everyone afterwards.'

Amy looked at her. It would be churlish to say nothing to this girl who was so important to Mitch, and who had done so much to ensure the future of Lavender.

She held out her hands. 'Jacey – you look wonderful,' she said sincerely.

'Thanks.' Jacey grasped Amy's hands in hers. 'So do you.'

Impulsively, Amy hugged her. 'Welcome to the family, love.'

'Thanks,' Jacey said again, this time more gruffly, and she turned her head away.

'Mum!' Megan laughed. 'Now look what you've done! You've made her cry!'

'I'll get some Buck's Fizz,' Sally put in brightly, 'and we'll drink a toast to the women of Lavender Lane!'

They did, laughing and teasing as Amy raised her glass.

'To the most glamorous ladies in Oxfordshire!'

'An' me!' Kim tugged at Amy's skirt.

'Oh, yes, and you, poppet!' Amy picked up her granddaughter. 'You're the prettiest of all!'

Megan wondered fleetingly how that morning's other bride was feeling, and laughed. Cicely would no doubt be coping with her impending wedding in her usual indomitable way.

Amy sat beside her and held her hand.

'Well, Mrs almost-Dolan, how are you feeling?'

Meg raised her eyebrows. 'I honestly feel calm and happy and excited. Actually I was just wondering about Gran!'

'She'll be fine,' Amy assured her. 'It's Sam I feel sorry for. And my mum and dad!'

Stella and Jim had happily accepted Cicely's invitation to be witnesses at her Milton St John Manor wedding, but only if it meant the entire party would be at the church in time for Megan and Luke's.

It had taken a lot of planning, but the four of them should arrive at the church ten minutes before the service.

'They're not flying in that rickety plane that Sam and Gran have bought, are they?' Megan asked. 'I know that's what Gran wanted to do ...'

'No!' Amy laughed. 'They were persuaded to save that bit of stunt flying for after their blessing. They should arrive in a rather swish Daimler ...'

'Car!' Kim announced and they all laughed.

'She's obviously got Lavender blood in her veins!' said Sally, hugging her.

'Car!' Kim said again, pointing to the window.

'Goodness!' Amy stood up. 'She's right. It's time for us to go, ladies.' She turned to look at Megan for the last time.

'Dad'll be here in a second. I'll see you in church – and thanks for everything, Meg. You're the best daughter in the world ...'

Meg squeezed her hand. 'Because I've got the best parents! You get the bridesmaids in the car and boss everyone around as befits the mother of the bride. Sally and Jacey will throttle you if you make me cry – they took hours with my make-up!'

'Mrs Webster!' Cicely sat back in the plush leather seats of the Daimler and linked her arm through Sam's, twisting her new wedding ring on her finger. 'It'll take some getting used to. And I suppose I'll always be Gran Phillips to the children ...' She looked anxiously at her new husband. 'You won't mind, will you?'

'Not at all,' Sam assured her. 'You'll still be my Cicely, whatever they call you! I'm the proudest and happiest man in the entire world, my love. I've waited a lifetime for this moment.'

Cicely stretched up and kissed his cheek.

'So have I. I've been doubly lucky ...'

Stella straightened her new hat – a wild confection in yellow and black, and one of the nicest she'd ever bought – and smiled at them.

'I never expected to be a bridesmaid again at my age, but I thoroughly enjoyed it! I wonder how the rest of them are coping? I must say, your wedding went without a hitch. I only hope this one does ...'

Cicely laughed. 'I'm sure it will. I doubt Megan and Luke will be nervous. I've never seen anyone more in love than those two – unless it was Bob and Amy. They never had eyes for anyone else, either.'

The Daimler swept along Appleford's main road towards the church, and as Saturday morning shoppers stopped to stare, Sam had to grip Cicely's hands tightly to prevent her giving them the benefit of a regal wave.

'The bridesmaids are all in the porch,' Stella announced as Jim helped her from the car. 'And there's Amy fussing around straightening dresses! Oh, this is such a happy day ...'

Following the others slowly up the mossy path to the church door, Sam caught hold of Cicely's hand and pulled her towards him.

'I know the rest of today will really belong to Meg and Luke, but I just wanted to say that I love you very, very much. To me you'll always be that crazy girl who strapped herself to the wings of my plane with such absolute trust.'

'And you'll always be the heart-stoppingly handsome young man to whom I entrusted my life,' Cicely said, for once serious. 'That's how you're going to stay, too.'

Fingers entwined, Mr and Mrs Webster walked forward to be enveloped in congratulations from Amy, the bridesmaids, and a stream of latecomers, before entering the cool peace of the church.

'Nervous?' Bob raised his eyebrows at Meg as their car pulled up. 'If you are, you certainly don't look it ...'

'I'm not.' Megan straightened her veil and clutched her bouquet of roses even tighter. 'I'm just very happy. But I'm going to miss you.'

'We'll miss you too, love.' Carefully he helped her from the car. 'Meg, you look simply lovely. I must be the proudest father in the world. Are you ready?'

She nodded as the photographer swooped. She could see Jacey, Sally, and Kim in the church porch and Luke would be waiting at the altar.

She linked her arm through her father's and smiled.

'I'm ready.'

They made their stately way up the aisle to where Luke and Mitch were waiting, then, his duties as father of the bride accomplished, Bob slid into the pew beside Amy and took her hand. He couldn't speak, but as they looked at each other, as ever they had no need for words, and she squeezed his hand in understanding.

Meg and Luke were taking their vows, their voices clear and steady under the vaulted roof. The sunlight threw gemstone patterns through the stained-glass windows on to the floor of the church, filled to capacity with family and friends.

Then the newly married couple stepped aside as Cicely and Sam walked forward to have their marriage blessed.

Amy moved closer to Bob. 'Isn't this wonderful?' she whispered, and he squeezed her hand.

It didn't seem possible that so many years had flown since he and Amy had taken their vows here, with his father conducting the service. How lucky they had been – and how right to decide to spend the rest of their lives simply being together.

The organ wheezed into life as the wedding party moved to the vestry, and Bob took Amy's hand.

'I was just thinking ...'

'That thirty years ago we were doing this?' Amy wiped away a tear. 'I know, darling, I know.'

The reception was in full swing. The Seven Stars had pulled out all the stops – after all, they had never had two brides and bridegrooms at the same function before – and once the speeches and toasts were out of the way, the cakes cut, and the jokes made, they had cleared the room for dancing.

A small room had been set aside for the more sedate members of the party to enjoy a cup of tea. Stella, refusing to remove her hat but blissfully kicking off her shoes, wriggled her toes.

'That was the best wedding Appleford has ever seen,' she said proudly. 'I wonder where everyone else is?'

Jim laughed. 'Meg and Luke are gazing at each other in complete disbelief. I think Cicely is already trying to get everyone to do the hokey-cokey – and Bob and Amy have disappeared.'

'It's been a bit of a day for them, hasn't it?' Stella observed. 'I expect they need some time to themselves.'

Gazing down into the little stream that trickled beneath the bridge, Bob and Amy were standing side by side in silent contentment. The wedding parties had spilled out of The Seven Stars and were dancing and talking, laughing and singing, on the lawn in the May sunshine.

Amy turned to lean her back against the worn handrail and lifted her face to the sun.

'There's only one fly in the ointment,' she murmured. 'Or

168

rather, two.'

'Paul and Judith?' Bob guessed. 'Yes, I'd be happier with those two out of the way, but there's nothing we can do about that. The kids'll have to do the best they can – and hope they don't interfere too much.'

Amy looked across the stream towards the lawn where Mitch, Jacey, Matt, Sally, and Kim were sitting making daisy chains, totally disregarding their finery, laughing together. Luke and Megan, their arms round each other, were dazedly accepting yet more congratulations, with eyes only for each other.

'With the money from the bank, and Sam's input, maybe they'll be persuaded to sell their shares one day,' Amy suggested hopefully, and Bob slid his arm round her shoulders.

'Maybe. Still, we don't need to worry about it now. Perhaps we could talk to them again before we leave for Starpoint.'

Amy nodded, then groaned as she caught sight of Judith and Paul hurrying across the lawn towards them.

'Oh, well, it couldn't all be perfect,' Bob teased her.

'Lovely wedding!' Judith blew air kisses and spoke as if it had been a complete surprise. 'Megan looked wonderful – and your mother is a picture, Bob! And the reception – well!'

'So glad you enjoyed it,' Amy said shortly. 'Although I'm sure that when your two get married you'll be looking for something far more sumptuous!'

'Oh, that won't be for ages yet!' Judith trilled. 'Paul and I feel far too young to think about this sort of thing. And as for being grandparents – well! It's positively ageing!'

'Nonsense! I love it,' Amy said. 'We both do. I hope Meg and Luke start a family soon, and that Kim has a brother or sister before long. The. more the merrier …'

'Each to his own, I suppose,' Paul said, trying to head off a further row between the sisters. 'Actually, Judith and I have something to tell you,' he added with a smile.

Judith, pleating the ends of her chiffon scarf, beamed.

'Yes, we've got some wonderful news. Paul and I have been offered a franchise for the Silver Bird Service Station and Diner on the Henley Road. It's an absolutely golden business opportunity – and far enough away from Lavender not to offer any competition!'

'It's everything we wanted for Lavender, and more,' Paul enthused. 'Of course, we'll have to sell our shares in Lavender at once. Obviously you and Bob don't want them now, so I wondered if Mitch and Megan would consider a deal?'

Amy bit her lips to prevent herself from laughing out loud.

'I'm sure they'll be willing to consider it,' she said shakily. 'You probably won't get much sense out of Meg at the moment, but I'm sure Mitch will be prepared to talk – especially as you want a quick decision. Why don't you speak to him?'

'We will.' Judith was already leading the way towards the lawn. 'Come along, Paul!'

As soon as they were out of earshot. Bob hugged Amy in delight.

'I only hope Mitch makes them grovel! He mustn't give in too easily.

Oh, what a wonderful day!'

'Wonderful!' Amy echoed. 'Simply the most perfect day of our lives!'

And they kissed in the warm May sunshine.

More titles by **Christina Jones**

For more information about **Christina Jones**
and other **Accent Press** titles
please visit

www.accentpress.co.uk

Lightning Source UK Ltd.
Milton Keynes UK
UKOW06n1922271115

263659UK00001B/4/P